THE PRINCESS GALVA
A ROMANCE

By
David Whitelaw

AUTHOR OF "THE GANG," "MOON OF VALLEYS," ETC.

"Romance is what is round the next bend of the road and across the horizon. Yesterday is romantic and so is to-morrow."—Professor Raleigh, at the London Institution.

Double 9
BOOKS

The Princess Galva-A Romance

by David Whitelaw

ISBN: 978-93-56567-66-5

Published by
DOUBLE 9 BOOKS
2/13-B, Ansari Road
Daryaganj, New Delhi – 110002
info@double9books.com
www.double9books.com
Tel. 011-40042856

Printed in India.

ABOUT THE AUTHOR

David Whitelaw was born to Hannah Baxter and David Whitelaw in Holloway, Islington, which was then part of Middlesex. His grandparents, Theodore and Eliza Baxter, members of the North London branch of the Sandemanian church, raised him and his older brother Stephen (1873 - 1936) after the death of both of their parents when they were both infants.

Following brief stays in New York City and Paris in the 1890s, Whitelaw returned to London to work as an illustrator and journalist for a number of Fleet Street publications. He subsequently rose to the position of editor of The London Magazine and The Premier Magazine. Between 1914 and 1931, the Amalgamated Press's The Premier Magazine, which was housed at Fleetway House in Farringdon, London, produced atmospheric fiction including action and mystery writers like Edgar Wallace.

He created the spelling card game Lexicon in 1932, which became very famous all over the world. In his lifetime, he published more than 50 books, and The Thriller magazine also ran serial versions of his stories. His first book, "M'Stodger's Affinity," was released in 1896, and a string of romantic suspense novels followed. Many of his works were translated into various languages and were published in multiple editions.

CONTENTS

CHAPTER I.

TOO OLD AT FORTY

The waning light of an October evening shone on the reflectors outside the windows of the basement counting-house, and the clerk at the corner desk could barely discern that the clock on the green painted dusty wall pointed to a quarter to six.

In fifteen minutes Edward Povey's twenty-two years of devoted service in the interests of Messrs. Kyser, Schultz & Company would come to an end, and the desk in the corner to which he had been promoted fifteen years ago would by the immutable law of evolution pass into the possession of his junior. Edward noticed this junior now and the glances which that young man cast at the scratched and ink-stained slab of mahogany that was to constitute his kingdom of the morrow. Edward wondered dully whether the young man was as full of hope as he himself had been. Perhaps he was waiting to be married even as he, Edward, had waited fifteen years ago. In those days the era of the Young Man had not been so pronounced as it is to-day, and it had been death that had removed his predecessor.

Even now he could remember the chastened sorrow with which he mounted the high stool of his desire. He had propped open the desk and collected together the belongings of the deceased clerk, and posted them with a little note of sympathy to his widow. Some had seemed too trivial to send, and of these a few still remained, a battered soap-box, a small square of unframed looking-glass, its red back scratched and scored. These, together with the great ebony ruler, had now outlasted his own reign and would pass to the new-comer.

And now the desk was propped open again, and it was his own belongings that he was collecting into a heap. The well-known odour of the wood came to his nostrils and he sighed a little. From shadowy and dusty corners he got together the little trifles that had been part and parcel of his life and arranged them in a neat pile beside him.

"If there's anything I can do for you——" began the junior, brushing his hair in front of a little mirror and settling his purple tie nervously.

"No, Joynings; nothing, I thank you. I'm leaving you old Brown's looking-glass and soap-box—they're fixtures, and go with the position."

The junior tittered a little at this and pulled down the front of his fancy waistcoat, lit a cigarette, and took a pair of roller-skates from the drawer of his desk. He came over and held out his hand.

"Right, then I'll be popping along—good luck, old man, and all that. You'll drop into something soon. If I hear of anything——"

"Oh, I'll be all right," said Edward Povey.

There is always a certain fascination in change and elation in abnormal conditions, even if those conditions constitute a misfortune. Edward Povey was surprised at his inner feelings as he left the portals of Messrs. Kyser, Schultz & Company's offices. In his own mind he knew that he ought to be feeling depressed; but the fact remained that he was feeling nothing of the kind, indeed he felt happier than he had done for the past twenty-two years, except perhaps on that one evening fifteen years ago. Then he had been hurrying out to a small house in a mean street in Barnsbury, to a little woman who was waiting for the news that would enable her to become the wife of the man who brought it. Now he was going to another little house in a mean street, in Clapham this time, to the same woman, but with how different tidings and how differently they would be received. Fifteen years ago the future had looked very bright to the limited vision of Mr. Edward Povey. He had left the office after his marriage with a light step and hurried across the bridge that would lead him to the villa he had taken. As the years passed, the light step had become a sedate walk, and now it was hard to recognize in the little bowed figure that shuffled each evening across London Bridge the Edward Povey of other days.

But to-night, curiously enough, the step was not shuffling and the little iron-grey head was more erect. The blow that had fallen when

Mr. Schultz had given him the buff envelope which contained his salary and his *congé* had been deadening, and the feeling had numbed him for the whole day. Then had come the inevitable reaction, the need for movement, for effort, and the heart of Edward Povey was responding nobly to the call, the heart that had lain dormant since the early days of his marriage.

For Charlotte Povey, estimable woman, cherished fondly the idea that for fifteen years she had been moulding the life, the destinies, and the character of her husband, and he, for the sake of peace, had given himself unresistingly to the potter's thumb. Charlotte's method, however, left much to be desired. With the laudable object of rousing the soul of Edward to further action and endeavour, she let not a day pass without comparing, much to his disparagement, his actions and even his appearance with other men of their acquaintance.

But instead of this having the desired effect, Edward had gradually come to believe it all; it had been so consistently impressed upon him that he was a poor sort of a chap anyway, and the inevitable result was—the envelope presented to him that morning by Mr. Schultz.

And now, on this calm autumn evening the chains of fifteen years fell from him and the spirit of Edward Povey underwent a change. He began to think that it was a good, full world—a world in which there were more things and higher possibilities than the evil-smelling counting-house of Kyser, Schultz & Company. He told himself that he had wasted nearly a quarter of a century.

The city was settling to quietude under a pall of smoky opal. The warehouses and buildings stood out gaunt and grey. The river flowing under the railway arches up-stream was splashed with the glory of the setting sun, little elusive reflections showing blood-red on the muddy water. Edward had crossed London Bridge for many years, but he did not remember ever having seen a sunset there.

Clapham! The world was bigger than Clapham.—Forty years of age! Why, it was the prime of a man's life, rather before the prime, in fact. Edward stopped, there was no hurry to-night, and leant over the parapet of the bridge. Below him, on the wharf, they were unloading a tramp steamer of boxes of fruit. The men swarming like ants up the long gangways were carrying on their backs light crates. One of these boxes had come apart and lay on the grimy deck shedding a little pool of golden oranges. The clatter of winches, the jangling of cranes, all served to make up a picture of life and movement that appealed strongly to the man who was leaning over the stone balustrade. He could read the name on the stern of the boat, "*Isabella – Barcelona*."

There were other boats too, and barges, huddling together as though for warmth like little chickens in an incubator. The bascules of the Tower Bridge, showing dimly in the haze, were being raised to let a white-funneled steamer that was cautiously sidling out into mid-stream slip down to the sea. Two men were working vigorously with long poles, guiding a barge laden with straw out of her way. Edward Povey watched her, telling himself that in a few hours she would be making her way down Channel or breasting the waves in the North Sea. Later she would be in some palm-fringed Southern port, or perhaps amid the romantic islands and fjords of the North.

He wished that he, too, could go abroad, that he too could slide out of London on the dingy bosom of Father Thames. He longed to breathe the large airs of the ocean, to feel the sting of the salt spray, and to reach the places blazoned so bravely forth in gold letters upon the sterns below him. Barcelona, for instance, spoke of sunny skies and indolence and romance, and he felt a great pity for the surging masses of which he had so lately been one, who pushed past him with never a glance for the river or the sunset, or for the *Isabella* from Barcelona.

A light tap on his shoulder brought him out of his reverie, to see the genial face of Mr. Kyser, the other partner of the firm to whom he had been correspondence clerk for so many years. Edward had never had much to do with the junior partner, but what small relations they had had seemed to be touched with more humanity than was the case with Mr. Schultz.

"— —and so you are leaving us, Mr. Povey?" Kyser was saying.

"Yes, sir, I— —"

"Well, Povey, I'm sorry, yes, I'm sorry; but there, I can't interfere with what Mr. Schultz does, it's his department, you know, but I didn't want to pass you without a handshake. Let me see, you live at Clapham, don't you?"

Edward Povey nodded.

"We'll get a taxi, then—or, better still, come and have a chop with me—I want a word with you."

Edward was delighted. Surely things were far better than they had been for a quarter of a century. Yesterday this same man would have passed him with perhaps a nod, perhaps not even that.

The change that had come over Edward since his release from bondage was evidently being sustained by events. For fifteen years he had passed the spacious grill-room in Gracechurch Street, with its noble array of chops and parsley in the window, in which he now found himself, on his way to the little eating-house up the court where he had taken his modest midday meal of sandwiches and stout. There was a sense of well-being about his present surroundings that gave him a feeling as though he had set foot in a new world and that he meant to remain in it. The snowy linen, the silver and glass, the little green-curtained alcoves, the obsequious waiters, the flickering and hissing of the grill at the further end of the room, presided over by the white-clad chef, all played their part in the awakening of Edward Povey.

"It's not much that I wanted to speak to you about, Povey, but I thought you might help me. You'll be looking round for another place, I suppose, but if you can find time to run out to Bushey now and again, you'll be obliging me—personally."

Edward Povey expressed his willingness to do all that lay in his power.

"It's only to have a look at my little cottage there, Povey; I've been living there on and off, and now I'm off to Switzerland. My man goes with me, so I want you to run out and see that things are all right. I'll give you the key. Any letters that come you can keep for me until my return. I've got a few decent pictures at the cottage and some old silver that I'm anxious not to leave altogether unattended. Can I count on you?"

Edward repeated his assurances, but a sense of disappointment had come over him as Kyser had been speaking. The adventure was not panning out as he had hoped. At the same time, he told himself that he would be paid for his services, perhaps liberally, and it might prevent him having to touch the little nest-egg in the Post Office Savings Bank.

When Edward parted with his late employer and left the grill-room it was with the key of Adderbury Cottage, Bushey Heath, in his pocket, and rather a feeling of resentment against Mr. Kyser and his firm, who did not hesitate to use a servant of twenty-two years' standing as a mere caretaker.

And resentment was a dangerous thing in the brain of the new Edward Povey.

CHAPTER II.

AT NO. 8, BELITHA VILLAS

It was nine o'clock when Edward Povey pushed open the little iron gate of No. 8, Belitha Villas, Clapham, thereby announcing his return to the other eleven villas in the same row. For the twelve little iron gates of Belitha Villas had each its own peculiar squeak and clang, a fact that added considerably to the scandal-mongering of the little community, and had caused a certain old reprobate at No. 3 to make liberal use of the oil-can.

The master of No. 8 let himself in with his latch-key, and groping his way down the dark and narrow passage pushed open the dining-room door. The room was in darkness save for a little evil-smelling oil-lamp which shed a dismal radiance upon a cloth spread half across the table. An unsympathetic slab of red topside of beef glared aggressively from a dish in which the gravy had set to an unhealthy-looking fat-ringed jelly. This, flanked by the remains of a cottage loaf and a glass of ale, constituted the meal that Charlotte had left for the refreshment of her lord and master. The ale had long been drawn, and stood dead and listless, showing a surface destitute of foam. Edward took one sip, then sat down and lit a cigarette.

His gaze wandered round the little room, the corners of which were in a dingy shadow, and contrasted it in his mind with the grill-room of the Blue Dragon. And then his eye lighted upon a letter propped up against the brass lamp and put there evidently so that it should attract his early attention. He took it up and read it through, then with a few uncomplimentary remarks he thrust it into his pocket and, taking up the lamp, made his way up-stairs. Another moment and he was back again, holding the lamp above his head and searching the dim corners of the room.

A large unwieldy form that had been stretched upon a sofa in the shadow of the window recess roused itself and sat upright. It was clad in a shabby dressing-gown of some dark material and it had a stern eye.

"You're late, Edward."

"Yes, my dear, I am a little, I think. I thought you were up-stairs or had run along to have a chat with Mrs. Oakley. I didn't see you in the shadow there."

"I saw *you*, Edward, and I saw you read the letter, and I—I heard what you called uncle, and I am not in the habit of running along and having a chat with my neighbours in the middle of the night."

"Well, my dear woman, I didn't know you were there when I read his letter or I wouldn't have said it,—and it's only nine o'clock."

"That's enough, Edward; you've said what you've said. I'm astonished, but it can't be mended; they say men speak their true thoughts when they're in drink."

"I beg your pardon, Charlotte, I——"

"I'm not angry, Edward, but don't bang the lamp down like that, you'll splash the oil out. I repeat I'm not angry, only sorry. When I see a man come home at this hour and turn up his nose at a glass of good honest ale I know what it means. But that doesn't excuse what you said about uncle."

"Well, he's a rotten nuisance. I know as well as you do that we can't afford to upset the old chap, but he shouldn't come down on us like this, especially——"

"Especially what——?"

"——especially when it's—it's not convenient. The fact is, Charlotte, we'll have to draw in our horns a bit. I've got the sack, my dear, the push—the bullet—after twenty-two years—curse 'em."

"Edward, you forget you're speaking to me."

"Oh, no, I don't, my dear. I'm talking exactly how I feel. I'll get even with 'em yet. I'm going to draw some fresh beer."

When Edward returned, Charlotte had lit the hanging lamp with the green shade over the centre of the table and had settled herself in the one saddle-bag chair. Her husband sat opposite to her on a shiny horsehair stool and poured out a glass of foaming ale.

"Your health, my dear," he said, and drank deep.

"Umph! you seem to take it coolly, Edward; I suppose you think it's the easiest thing in the world to get employment at your age. Look at Mr. Hardy at No. 4, out for fifteen months and speaks Portuguese, they say, like a native——"

Edward held up a protesting hand.

"Mr. Hardy, my dear, doesn't enter into this. What's happened to-day has made me do a bit of hard thinking. Forty's not old, Charlotte, it's young. I feel like a boy just let out of school. I'll be full of schemes in a day or two."

Mrs. Povey waved her hands unconvincedly.

"But the present," she remarked with a sinister sweetness. "I suppose that hasn't entered into your head, eh? How about uncle? he's a self-made man and thinks everyone should succeed. When he hears you're sacked he'll cut us off without the shilling. He always says he's got no use for failures."

Mrs. Povey paused, and getting no reply went on.

"Besides, I've written to Aunt Eliza plenty of times and said how well we were doing; in fact, I'm afraid I've exaggerated, and now, here he is coming to visit us. I'm afraid he'll have a sort of awakening—and so will we."

Sitting forward with his hands on his knees, Edward Povey was staring into the little heap of cinders in the heart of which still glowed a dull red. His lips were parted and his eyes were dilated. Mrs. Povey leant over and shook him roughly by the shoulder. Then she moved the jug of beer out of his reach.

"Edward Povey, ain't you ashamed of yourself—the state you're in—go to bed—you hear me?"

Her husband drew his eyes from the contemplation of the fire and motioned to his wife to sit down.

"It's working out," he said, and stretched out his hand for the jug that wasn't there. Then he cleared his throat and told his wife about his adventure of the evening. Charlotte listened in a forbidding silence, and when he had finished:

"I don't know what all this gallivanting about in restaurants has to do with me," she said sharply, "a few shillings a week—it'll hardly pay your fare."

"One moment, dear? You say that uncle comes to us on Monday—you know what his visits are, only business trips, and at the most he'll stay two nights. And, Charlotte, Mr. Kyser goes to Switzerland to-morrow for a month—see?"

"See what?"

"My dear Charlotte, I've always thought that women as a class are inferior to us men, but for sheer unadulterated stupidity and criminal density commend me to Charlotte Povey."

"Edward—you dare to——"

"Dare, my dear, I dare anything. Fifteen years of being compared to Brown, Jones and Robinson and Hardy is enough, madam. The men you have thrown in my face are worms, Charlotte, *worms*. I dare anything," he repeated, and walked round the table and recovered the jug.

"Now listen, Charlotte," he went on more quietly, when he had reseated himself. "I said that uncle is coming to us on *Monday*, and that Kyser goes to Switzerland or Sweden, or somewhere *to-morrow*."

Mrs. Povey was leaning back in her chair, her eyes closed to denote that to her at least the proceedings had lost all interest. Something, however, in the tone of her husband's voice brought her sharply to herself.

"Bushey is a fine place, nice and high, and healthy, Charlotte, and will suit uncle down to the ground. He'll find us living there in style—it'll impress him—and——"

"Edward! are you mad? Bushey—we don't live at Bushey."

Her husband smiled sarcastically.

"Don't we, my dear? really you surprise me—but we're going to, Charlotte, we're going to—for two nights only, as the play-bills say. We are going to *borrow* Adderbury Cottage. The firm owes me a bit, and I›ll take it out in Adderbury Cottages.»

Charlotte was fully roused now.

"Edward Povey, I'll not do it."

Her husband brought his fist down on the table with a thump that rattled the crockery and even infused a little flickering life into the surface of the glass of dull supper beer.

"You'll do as I say, Charlotte; I'm master here now, and new brooms sweep clean, you know. Now, put some more coals on, and go to bed."

With a strange sense of awe Mrs. Povey, for the first time in her married life, did as she was bid, and, with a look of wonderment on her vacant face, glided slowly from the room. For perhaps another hour Edward sat over the replenished fire elaborating his scheme. Really it was absurdly simple; of risk there was none. A kind fate had shown them a simple way out of their difficulties, and it would be criminal to ignore it. He knew Uncle Jasper far too well to think of admitting to him that he was a failure in the world. He knew, too, that the old man held him in some little contempt, and he welcomed this chance of showing him his mistake. As for Charlotte, she had evidently committed herself pretty deeply in her correspondence with Aunt Eliza, and Edward anticipated no sustained opposition from that quarter.

It was past midnight when Edward rose and opened the little fumed oak bureau that stood in the recess by the fire-place, and taking a sheet of the notepaper of Messrs. Kyser, Schultz & Company, wrote to Mr. Jasper Jarman telling him how glad Charlotte and himself were to hear that he proposed paying them a visit. He said that the firm for which he had the honour to work had at last awakened to the value of his services, and that a substantial increase of salary had given him the opportunity to receive his dear wife's uncle in a manner more fitted to his position, and that he remained with all good wishes, his uncle's most affectionate nephew, Edward Povey.

The little iron gate creaked again that night, and as Edward dropped the letter into the box at the corner of the terrace he told himself that his new life promised infinitely more possibilities than that to which he had been accustomed for the past fifteen years.

CHAPTER III.

BORROWED PLUMAGE

The word *phew* may have a somewhat indefinite position in the English language, but there was no mistaking the tone in which Mr. Edward Povey said it as he sank wearily into the depths of one of the handsome green leather chairs that stood on either side of the fireplace in the dining-room at Adderbury Cottage, Bushey Heath. The tone of the ejaculation plainly indicated escape, or at any rate temporary relief from a severe nerve-racking strain.

At the further side of the table beneath the great crimson shaded lamp sat Charlotte, her fingers drumming a nervous tattoo upon the polished black oak beneath them. She, too, like her husband showed signs of severe nervous prostration. She raised her head as though about to answer Edward's ejaculation but sighed instead and fell again to her incessant tapping.

"Do stop that infernal row, Charlotte; you sit there and tap, tap, tap, as though—as though—well, give it a rest, it's getting nervy," then after a pause, "where have you put them?"

"Them?"

"Yes,—our honoured guests—making themselves at home, aren't they? Have you noticed, Charlotte, that there's been no mention of how long they're going to stay?"

"I've put them in the room above this. I expect it's old Kyser's room when he's at home here, all chintz and Sheraton."

Edward Povey sat silent for a few moments, gazing stolidly into the fire that was burning brightly in the old-fashioned fire-place. Then he got up and with hands thrust deep in his pockets strode up and down the room, his steps making no sound on the rich turkey carpet.

"It's going to be rather a harder job than I thought, Charlotte," he said at length, pausing in his walk and staring gloomily down at his wife, "so many things have turned out differently to what we thought. Why couldn't the old fool have said he was bringing Aunt Eliza? she's never come before when he's paid us a visit. I thought I should have fainted dead off just now when the old fellow asked me to show him which was the bath-room—he takes a cold tub every morning. Fancy not knowing where the bath-room is in one's own house. I had to open every door I came to and call out 'puss'—said I was looking for a kitten we'd lost—until I came to the right one, the fifth door I opened I think it was."

Edward passed his handkerchief over his forehead, then resumed.

"I blame you, Charlotte, for the unfortunate affair of the photo album. You should have put the book out of sight like you did the framed photos. I can't understand old Kyser keeping such a book full of crocks anyway, I'd be frightened to death of blackmail. You ought to have known that albums are Aunt Eliza's special weakness. She got hold of it at once and made me go through all the lot and tell her who they were and all about them." Edward grew hot at the remembrance. "It isn't easy to invent names and plausible histories for an assorted lot like that at a moment's notice—ugly lot of devils, too."

"The whole idea is yours remember, Edward."

"I know that, woman. Do you think it makes it any easier for me?—you shouldn't have let me—you——"

"You forget, Edward, you said that you were to be master in your own house."

"This *isn't* my own house, is it? But look here, Charlotte, it›s not the least bit of good our arguing how we came to be here. We are here, and here we've got to stay and make the best of a bad job. All we need is a little bit of coaching in some of the minor details. Come over here."

Edward took up a richly chased candelabra and led the way to the fire-place. He removed the little paper shades and let the light fall full upon the portrait of an aged and benevolent-looking gentleman in a splendid old English gilt frame.

"See him, Charlotte; I thought all dinner time your uncle was going to ask who he was. He's sure to ask to-morrow, inquisitive old idiot, and we've got to be prepared. Listen. This old chap here is a Mr. Tobias Kenwick—that doesn't sound faked, does it?—not like Brown or Smith. If uncle asks what he was, say he was an engineer and that he's now retired and living in Peru. This old lady over the sideboard," went on Edward, crossing the room, "can be a friend of my mother's; say she's been dead some years now and that you forget her name but think it was Jane something. Any other portraits he asks about say we picked them up at a sale. By the bye, I must congratulate you on your excuse for the absence of the servant—the dying sister in the North of Scotland was an inspiration. I'd trot off to bed now, Charlotte my dear, if I were you. I'll be up presently. I've got a bit of hard thinking to get through here before *I* think of sleep.»

Left to himself Edward ruminated deeply on the situation in which he had placed himself. Things had not turned out at all as he had expected and dilemmas had crowded thickly and fast upon him. The advent of Aunt Eliza had entirely unnerved him, and the amount of luggage which he had helped to take up to the bedroom seemed to him to be quite unnecessary for a short visit such as he had anticipated. Hitherto the visits of Uncle Jasper had been always the same, a night or two at the most and the days spent in business in London. His luggage had been invariably one suit case and a hatbox. But the present visit pointed more to a prolonged holiday than to a business trip. Edward tried to tell himself that there was nothing to fear, that Kyser would not return for a month, and that the secluded position of Adderbury Cottage was all in favour of the scheme; detection from the outside was a very remote chance.

Edward Povey, however, had not reckoned upon keeping the deception up for more than a few days at the most, neither had he reckoned upon the nerve strain. Tradesmen would be calling for orders—visitors, too, might reasonably be expected. A host of new possibilities arose before the perplexed vision of Edward Povey.

He could, of course, tell all comers that Mr. Kyser had lent him the house furnished. It was merely a small place used at intervals only by its wealthy owner. What more reasonable than that he should place it at the disposal of a friend? If he were alone, the guarding of the secret would be a simple matter, but there was Charlotte to complicate matters—Charlotte, who would innocently enough, by a chance word, upset his most carefully constructed fabrications.

From the hall came, the rich muffled chimes of a steel-faced Sheraton clock. It was midnight, and Edward rose, and crossing to the massive sideboard poured himself out a liberal allowance of brandy, splashing into the glass a little soda-water from a wired seltzogene. Then he proceeded to lock up.

Before barring the front door, he passed out on to the verandah-like porch and running his fingers through his thinning hair let the cool winds of the autumn night play upon the furnace of his forehead. It was very dark and the scene was desolate in the extreme. A solitary light twinkled out here and there from some window in the little village that lay beneath him in the valley, and farther off the pale radiance in the sky denoted the position of the town of Watford. There was a thick shrubbery encircling the house, and the masses of foliage took weird shapes in the darkness, and from a clump of gaunt fir-trees came the dismal note of an owl.

Edward Povey shivered a little, and, quietly closing the door, crept to his bed.

CHAPTER IV.

A LETTER FROM NEW YORK

Jasper Jarman was a self-made man, and, like many another self-made man, had a very exalted opinion of his own handiwork.

During his early career Jasper had fought a bitter battle with the world; by thirty-five he had conquered it, and now in the evening of his days he was very averse to relinquishing any of the moral spoils of his victory. To thwart Jasper Jarman was to rouse to their uttermost those fighting instincts that had given him the name of "Stone-wall Jarman" in his younger days.

Another trait common to self-made men was possessed by Jasper, he was an early riser. On the morning following his arrival at Adderbury Cottage he was abroad by seven, pacing up and down the trim box-bordered walk that ran round two sides of the house. He walked with an assertive tread, his large square-toed boots crunching the gravel rhythmically. His hands were lightly clasped behind his back, and with chest thrown well out he was inhaling the scented airs that rose from the dew-drenched garden. A blackbird strutted about the little lawn, and a close observer would have noticed a certain resemblance in the manners of man and bird.

From a little diamond-paned window a blind was drawn aside a few inches and an eye peeped cautiously forth upon the world. As the pompous figure of Mr. Jasper Jarman rounded the corner of the house and came into view, the blind was quickly dropped back into its place.

Five minutes later Edward Povey emerged from the front door, his unbuttoned waistcoat and his vaguely tied cravat giving the lie direct to the studied indifference of his walk.

His surprise at coming face to face with Mr. Jasper Jarman was quite an admirable piece of acting.

"Good-morning, Uncle Jasper; up with the lark, eh! the early bird, you know. Slept well, I hope?"

"Ah, Edward, my boy, good-morning—slept like a top, thanks; capital room Charlotte's given us. I'm afraid we've turned you out."

"Oh not at all, uncle, pray don't mention it."

"Faces east, though; your aunt finds the morning sun rather trying. She's going to turn the room out to-day and shift the bed to the other wall."

"Turn out the room, uncle?"

"Yes, my boy; capital woman your aunt, never idle a moment, always up and doing. You won't know this house after she's been here a month."

Edward thought it far more probable that it was the house that wouldn't know him by then, but, too taken aback to reply, he merely passed his handkerchief over his dry lips and waited for Jasper to continue.

The old man paused in his walk and ran his eye critically over some standard rose trees, that, each in its little island of mould, studded the lawn.

"Yes, my boy, you'll find we're not drones. We're busy bees, your aunt and me; what she does to the house I do to the garden. I'm never happy unless I'm pottering about with a trowel. I'll have this place," he waved his arm comprehensively, "shipshape in no time. I'll have those roses up and put 'em in a row under the window, they're wasted where they are, and we'll re-turf the lawn and make it big enough for croquet."

Jasper looked at Edward Povey for approbation. "Or even tennis," said the latter, who felt he must say something. Then he sat down on a rustic garden seat and nervously rolled himself a cigarette. Jasper, leaning a fat elbow upon the stone sundial, went on.

"A nice little place all the same, yes, a nice little place. Better than Clapham, eh, Edward?"

"Much better, uncle Jasper."

"The firm seems to have found out your worth at last. Well, I'm glad of it. Your aunt is always telling me that Charlotte married a fool—no, don't get angry, that's only her way of putting it. Been here long?"

"Not very long, uncle. You see, I've only got on lately. I discovered a scheme whereby my firm could save a small fortune in postage, and they rewarded me liberally. Then they found out I could correspond and speak in French and Spanish, so they rewarded me again. Oh! They've done me very well, I—— There's the gong for breakfast; we'll go in."

The meal was hardly a pleasant one. Aunt Eliza, whose temper the battle with the morning sun had not improved, munched her toast in silence. She was one of those individuals who appear to undergo a refrigerating process during the night hours and to awake frost-bitten. During the day she would gradually thaw. The process was sometimes rapid, but more often than not the midday dinner passed before Mrs. Jasper Jarman was even commonly polite. She had never been known to smile before eleven.

At eight-thirty Edward prepared to leave the house, presumably for the business offices of Messrs. Kyser, Schultz & Company, in Eastcheap. He was glad to escape from the charged atmosphere of the Adderbury Cottage dining-room, but he hated to leave Charlotte alone to play his game for him. To let Uncle Jasper suspect that he was not still in the service of the firm would of course be fatal. As he stood in the hall drawing on his gloves he noticed that the postman had left in the box a blue envelope. Making sure he was alone, he drew it out. It was, of course, addressed to Mr. Kyser, and Edward was about to place it unopened in his pocket, when his uncle's voice came from the stairs above—

"That for me, Edward?"

"No, uncle; it's—mine."

Mr. Jasper Jarman was descending the stairs, and, acting upon impulse, Edward inserted his thumb beneath the flap and slit open the envelope. The action was quite unpremeditated, but he thought it might look suspicious to place it in his pocket unopened when he had given Uncle Jasper to believe it was his own. He seemed to have an idea that his uncle would ask to see it.

Edward glanced at the clock, and, with a hurried good-bye, flew down the garden path, the open envelope still in his hand. On turning a bend of the road that hid him from view, he looked long and searchingly at it. It had been forwarded to Adderbury Cottage from Mr. Kyser's town house in Grosvenor Square, and Edward thought it strange that that should be so. Surely his housekeeper in town knew that her master was not at the cottage. Altogether Kyser's departure was rather suspicious. Edward had heard Mr. Schultz speaking to his partner the day he had left, had even heard them bid each other good-night, and now, as he thought of it, he remembered Schultz making an appointment for the next day. Looking at the affair squarely, it came home to Edward that Kyser's departure was hurried, not to say suspicious, and was even unknown to his housekeeper and his partner.

Suppose the owner of Adderbury Cottage had committed some crime, the police might even now be there after him. Self-preservation told Edward that he should read the contents of the envelope he held in his hand. Any information that showed light upon the situation it was clearly to his interest to know.

By this time he was walking rapidly down Clay Hill leading to the village of Bushey. He passed through the straggling High Street, past the old church, and descended the further hill into Watford. He was still holding in his hand the letter. At eleven o'clock he entered the smoking-room of the Rose and Crown, and having ordered a small Bass, drew a sheet of paper from the envelope that had been forwarded to Mr. Kyser from his town house in Grosvenor Square.

"19, WEST TWENTY-THIRD STREET,
"NEW YORK CITY,
"U.S.A.

"To Sydney Kyser, Esq.

"MY DEAR OLD FRIEND,

"You will be surprised to hear from me again after so long a lapse, but many things — ill-health among them — have prevented my travelling to England, although I have promised myself the trip many times in the past few years. And now I feel that I shall never take it, and that the doctor here, who gives me two weeks to live, speaks the truth. Well, I've had a good innings, and, as they say over

here, 'there's no kick coming.' I leave only one regret, and it is with regard to this that I venture to write to you. If you would do a dying man a kindness, and at the same time right a wrong, the chance is now yours. My state of health will not allow of my writing my request in full — and I ask you to promise nothing until you know all. This you can do by calling upon Mr. Abraham Nixon, 5A, St. Mary Axe, in the City of London.

"This gentleman will tell you a story so remarkable that it may seem to you incredible.

"But it is true every word of it. You will then act as you see fit. But I conjure you, by our past friendship, to do as Mr. Nixon asks.

"Your bona fide will consist of the crest torn from the head of this notepaper, which please send in to Mr. Nixon with these words written on it in red ink —

'MR. SYDNEY re GALVA'

"If you follow these instructions to the letter, Mr. Nixon will at once put you in complete possession of all the facts of the case.

"With my last breath I shall pray for you and the success of the mission.

"Yours,

   "HUBERT BAXENDALE.

"P.S. — You will see that Mr. Nixon will know you as Mr. Sydney. Not knowing whether you would like to undertake what I ask in your own name, I thought it wiser that in this matter you should be known simply as 'Mr. Sydney.'

"H. B."

Edward read the letter through many times before he finally folded it and replaced it in its envelope. Then he sat for a long time thinking on what he had read. There was no way of corresponding with Mr. Kyser for a month, and by that time the wrong that the letter spoke of might be past the righting.

Would it not be better if he were to act, as it were, for Mr. Kyser, and, under the name of Sydney, gather what information he could from Mr. Nixon? He would then be able to judge more clearly what it were best to do.

Of course, in his own mind, Edward knew well that to act as he suggested to himself was taking a most unwarrantable liberty with another's affairs; but he was hardly himself. The excitement of the last few days had had anything but a salutary effect upon his moral balance; he had been living in a hot-bed of lies, and his discriminating powers of right and wrong had deteriorated sadly.

Who could say but that in this letter was a way out of the hideous mess he had made of things up at Adderbury Cottage? There was nothing against his going to St. Mary Axe. The letter plainly showed that Mr. Kyser and Mr. Nixon were unacquainted. There would be nothing to tell him from the real Mr. Sydney. It would at least fill in the time during which he must remain away from the cottage.

Edward Povey called the waiter and borrowed a time-table. He consulted this, then made his way to the writing-room, where he found a bottle of red ink. From the head of Mr. Baxendale's letter he tore the crest and heading, and across it he wrote the words mentioned in the letter. This he folded and placed in his pocket-book.

At half-past three the same afternoon Mr. Edward Povey, *alias*, for the moment, Mr. Sydney, pushed open the swing doors of Mr. Abraham Nixon's office in St. Mary Axe—and came to grips with Romance.

CHAPTER V.

AN ECHO OF A TRAGEDY AND THE DRAINAGE OF A COTTAGE

As Edward was, after sending in his slip of paper, ushered into the private office, a tall, gaunt man of unmistakable solicitor type rose from his desk and crossed over to him with extended hand. Edward put his out also and winced somewhat as it was tightly engulfed by the bony fingers of the solicitor.

"Mr. Sydney, I understand."

Edward Povey bowed, he had no great liking for telling lies and he preferred to act them where possible.

Mr. Abraham Nixon handed a chair to his visitor, and, reseating himself at his desk, picked up a telephone receiver and inquired for Mr. Crooks, asking that gentleman to kindly be sure that they were not disturbed for at least one hour.

At this Edward grew cold with apprehension. It seemed to him that there was something of an ordeal in front of him. Mr. Nixon's first words, however, somewhat reassured him.

"I understand from Mr. Baxendale that you are entirely ignorant of the subject referred to in his letter, Mr. Sydney."

"Entirely, Mr. Nixon, and it is perhaps better to say at once that, however much I desire to help my old friend and to fall in with his wishes, I cannot hold myself liable in any way—cannot commit myself."

Mr. Nixon held up a thin hand.

"A very sensible remark, Mr. Sydney, and one that I should have made myself had I been placed as you are. You are not in any way bound by what I am telling you except in the event of your refusal; in which case I shall enjoin you to secrecy. Pray excuse me a moment."

Selecting a flat key from a ring he took from his pocket, Mr. Nixon left the room, returning in a few minutes with a small deed-box on which was painted in white letters—

GALVA—BAXENDALE

This, Mr. Nixon placed upon a small side table, and selecting a flat key from the bunch on his ring inserted it in the lock.

"It is a curious story that I have to tell you, Mr. Sydney," he began as he pushed open the creaking lid. "I suppose I'm the only person to whom Mr. Baxendale told it. A very reserved and secretive man, Mr. Sydney."

"Very," answered Edward Povey, much relieved to hear it. Then he kept silent as he watched the solicitor remove from the box a few small articles, each carefully sealed up and docketed in a neat handwriting, the purport of which Edward could not make out at the distance. These articles arranged in a row upon his desk, Mr. Nixon leant back in his chair, and, placing the tips of his thin fingers together, began his tale.

"Perhaps you will remember, Mr. Sydney, the era of bloodshed and murder which attacked the little island kingdom of San Pietro some years back, I think in the autumn of '93. It was, in its way, as virulent as the Paris revolution, but San Pietro is a small kingdom, and although quite independent was not able to withstand the pressure of her more powerful neighbours. Spain, being the nearest, has always had a word to say in the San Pietro politics. The result was that the crisis was as short-lived as it was terrible. The reigning family had been put to death at the outburst of the revolution. The king, rather a pleasure-loving sort of person, had enjoyed some popularity among his subjects, but his marriage with an actress whom he had met in Vienna inflamed the ladies of the court, and, through them, their husbands.

"Most of these were officers standing high at court or in the army, and considering their wives insulted by the presence of an actress upon the throne, planned the assassination under the cloak of politics. The result was the terrible doings at the Palace at Corbo on that night in October.

"Baxendale, then a middle-aged man, traveling on business in Spain at the time, took ship across to San Pietro, intending to send first-hand news to a paper he was interested in in New York. Once arrived, however, he found more difficulty in returning. The Dictator whom the people had set up was very rigid in the matter of censorship, and not only could poor Baxendale get no news through, but he himself was politely but firmly told he could not leave the island.

"One afternoon about three or four days after the massacre he was taking a walk through the Sebastin Park, which I understand is on the edge of the capital, and merges from cultivation to the wild track of forest land which lies to the north. Baxendale had walked further than he had intended and was surprised to find of a sudden that the sun was sinking. As he turned to retrace his steps a curious sound came to his ears, that was for all the world like the cry of a child, The forest at this place was very dense, the branches of the tall pines interlacing overhead, whilst the undergrowth was thick enough to hide objects at a few yards.

"Baxendale parted the bushes and forced a way through them in the direction from which the cries seemed to come. The wailing had stopped, and he was telling himself that it was some forest beast he had heard when it was again taken up, and now he made out the low crooning of one who hushes and soothes a baby. At this he moved faster, and in a few moments came upon a tumble-down hut such as is used by the charcoal-burners of the woods.

"He had not been heard, for the crooning still continued and was evidently having the desired effect, as the child's cries had ceased. His light tap at the crazy-hinged door was answered only by the sudden cessation of the voice, and a dead silence. Then he cautiously pushed open the door.

"It was a poor enough place—indeed, little more than a ruin, and, in the dim light, Baxendale told me he could not at first make out any definite object. As his eyes grew more accustomed to the gloom, however, he made out the figure of a woman. She was standing facing him; he could not see her face clearly, but her whole attitude was one of defiance, and she seemed to be standing at bay, guarding something behind her. Baxendale could make out a bench on which were rolled a few clothes.

"Just then a ray of the setting sun pierced the branches and illuminated the interior of the hut. On the heap of clothes was a little baby girl about two years of age. The red rays played round the curly head, and Baxendale was smitten to the heart as he looked from the sleeping babe to the woman, who, seeing in Baxendale a friend, had sunk down on the earth floor and was silently weeping."

Mr. Nixon paused, and cleared his throat. He looked at his listener for signs of attention. The latter, who had almost forgotten the part he was playing, in his interest in the tale that was being told to him, nodded his head and asked if Mr. Nixon objected to tobacco. The two men smoked for a few moments in silence, then the solicitor resumed the tale.

"Beyond this I know very little and that little I will tell quickly. Baxendale came into this office in the spring of '98 and told me all this. The little child on wakening had held up her arms to him and smiled. The good fellow could not withstand the mute appeal, and resolved then and there that she should be his charge. Afterwards, when he had got them safely across to England, the woman who was the child's nurse told him the history. She had been afraid to do so earlier for fear it would have altered Baxendale's intentions, and she was too anxious to set her back to San Pietro to risk that.

"The baby girl was the Princess Miranda, only child of the ill-fated king and queen of San Pietro. On the fatal night, the nurse told Baxendale, she had been in the night nursery with the princess and her own niece, little Miranda's foster-sister, a child only a few months older than the princess. She told him of how she had seen the flare of torches and heard the clamour, and how the distracted queen had rushed in shrieking for her baby, and had caught up what she thought was her little one, and with it under her robe had fled to what she fondly considered was a place of safety.

"As events proved, there was no place of safety for that unhappy woman that night, and when the next day the bodies were laid to rest in the royal vault, a little dead child was buried with the queen, but it was not the Princess Miranda, although the monument that was raised by the tardy conscience of the San Pietro people is engraved with her name.

"Since the revolution, the political state of San Pietro has been somewhat uncertain. The people are simple and loyal folk at heart, and it was not long before they discovered the real reason of the uprising. Then they cried loudly for a king again, and Spain, who had only been waiting for this, put Prince Enrico upon the throne. You will have heard of this man, whose follies and deviltries are the talk of Europe. San Pietro tolerates him, for his court is brilliant, and has brought much money to the place; in fact, the whole island, and more especially the capital, is now one of the pleasure centres of Europe. This has had a most beneficent effect upon the fortunes of the island, but there are still some of the more sedate families who deplore the loss of dignity of their beloved land.

"The rightful heir is of course Miranda, the little princess with whom the poor nurse sought refuge in the forest.

"She is now living in England, the nurse is still with her, and Miranda has no idea of her high birth. Baxendale never confided to me what his projects were."

The solicitor leant over and picked up a letter which had been in the deed-box and handed it over to Edward, who took it and sat with it unopened in his hand waiting for Mr. Nixon to speak.

"You will read that when you leave here, Mr. Sydney, carefully, and I shall expect to hear from you in the course of a few days. There is the matter of money to be considered. My client has made adequate provision"—Edward pricked up his ears at this—"for what he terms 'the mission.'"

"In two days I will call on you again, Mr. Nixon. Good-afternoon."

Povey stood in Leadenhall Street at the entrance to St. Mary Axe and tried to think things over. It seemed to him as though he had just emerged from the gloom of romantic forests and the splendour of courts, and the foggy atmosphere and hoard of hurrying clerks appeared to him to be unreal. Then he pulled himself together and strolled quietly westward.

Along Leadenhall Street and through the market he walked deep in thought, making his way from force of habit in the direction of London Bridge. It was not until the spars and masts of the shipping came in sight that he remembered his changed conditions, when he hailed a passing taxi and was driven to Euston.

He had not long to wait for a train to Bushey, and no sooner had it left the platform than he had the letter out of his pocket and was breaking the seal. It was written on the paper of the Waldorf Hotel, New York, and was dated at the beginning of the year.

"MY DEAR SYDNEY,

"I am addressing you in this letter, as I hope and devoutly trust that yours will be the hands into which it will fall. My own health has been so bad of late and has shown such unmistakable signs of breaking up that I fear I must give up all hope of ever carrying out, personally, my desires. Next to myself, I would wish you to do so; failing you, Mr. Nixon has his instructions what to do. But you won't fail me.

"This gentleman will have told you the outlines of the history of the Princess Miranda. It has always been my desire that on her eighteenth birthday she should be told the story of her high origin. As this date approaches — the 15th of November — I feel that the seven or eight months between us will see my finish, so while there is yet time I write to you, my old friend, to act for me in this matter.

"The Princess, I have named her Galva, after a carn in the vicinity of her house, is at present living with her nurse at Tremoor, a few miles from Penzance.

"Mr. Nixon will give you, on your expressing your willingness to undertake the mission, two or three objects which will prove beyond doubt the claim of the dear girl to the throne of San Pietro. You will go to her and tell her everything; I would not feel I had done my duty were I to keep her in ignorance, although it might be kinder to do so.

"If, after hearing you out, she elects to remain in her quiet peaceful life, she shall do so. If, on the other hand, she decides on following up her high destiny you will take her with her nurse to Corbo, travelling as independent English tourists, and seek out Señor Luazo, or his heir, at 66, Calle Mendaro, and hand him a letter which Mr. Nixon will give you. After that I can safely leave you in his keeping.

"My fortune, I have divided equally between the man who undertakes this mission and Galva herself, with the exception of an annuity to Señora Paluda, the nurse who has done so much and been so much to little Galva.

"I can easily throw my mind back to that day in the forest, and the smiling babe holding up her little arms is a picture that will always

*be with me even at the end. Tell Galva that I will die thinking of her
and of all she has been to a lonely old bachelor.*

*"When the end comes, too, I will think of you and of what you are
doing for me, and will bless you for it.*

"And now, my old friend, good-bye.

"Yours ever,

HUBERT BAXENDALE."

Edward Povey folded up the letter carefully and placed it in his
pocket. Then, leaning his head in his hand, gazed out at the flying
landscape and tried to think things out. It took him some little time to
appreciate who he really was.

He had felt, ever since Mr. Nixon had mentioned the financial
aspect of the undertaking, that he would be more than foolish to let
slip such a providential way out of his sea of difficulties. The moral
side to the question he was able to smooth over to his satisfaction.
He knew Mr. Kyser, and Mr. Kyser's ways, and told himself that that
gentleman would not welcome, at his time of life, an adventure such
as the one that the solicitor had put before him that afternoon. Again,
he told himself that it was not possible for him to communicate with
Mr. Kyser until the eighteenth birthday of the princess had passed.
He said it would be wrong and unkind to let the poor lonely girl think
that she was forgotten.

Further self-discussion on the matter was taken out of his hands by
a watching Fate who suggested something refreshing as he breasted
the first part of the straggling hill that led from the railway station
up to Bushey Heath. He paused at the Merry Month of May, then
decided to push on to a little hostelry that he had noticed on the way
down that morning.

He entered the door of the White Hart and turned to the right
through the tiny bar into the smoke-room. Two tweed-clad artists
from the near-by studios lounged in more or less elegant poses at the
red-clothed table, they looked up and nodded as Edward entered, then
returned to the perusal of the evening papers which had evidently
just arrived.

The host of the inn came from the bar and attended to the new-
comer's wants, and Edward took from his pocket an *Evening News* that
he had bought in town. He read it listlessly for some minutes, then

the two bored-looking youths looked up suddenly as the man gave a gasp. They stared at him so curiously that he felt an explanation was necessary.

"Went the wrong way—gentlemen," he said, pointing to his glass of beer—"windpipe, I think."

The elder of the two youths grunted and leaning back lit a cigarette. He watched Edward, at first carelessly, but as he saw the man take out a penknife and cut from the paper a paragraph, he grew more interested. In a few moments Edward gulped down his beer, and, without a word, made his way outside.

"Bertie," it was the elder artist who was speaking, "that chap saw something in the paper that upset him a little—is that the *News* you›re reading?»

"Yes—why?"

"Look at page five, will you, the third paragraph from the bottom on column two. Read it out loud if you don't mind."

The paper rustled as the other young man turned to the desired portion, then in a blasé voice read:—

"MYSTERIOUS DEATH IN PARIS.

"A gentleman who arrived at the Hôtel Meurice from London two days ago has met with a fate such as is becoming more and more frequent in the streets of Paris. A gendarme passing down the Rue des Batignolles last evening about ten o'clock, came upon the body of the unfortunate man huddled into an angle of a doorway. Assistance was forthcoming, but was too late to be of any service to the victim, who had suffered terrible injuries to the head, and to which he succumbed within an hour after his admission to the hospital. The outrage points undoubtedly to being the work of the dreaded Apaches. The deceased gentleman, who was about fifty years of age, had registered under the name of Sydney Kyser, but it has been impossible to trace among his belongings any clue to his home address. The French police, however, are in communication with Scotland Yard, and are in the mean time actively engaged in searching for the perpetrators of the outrage."

"Bet you that chap knew this Kyser, or whoever it is——" a yawn—"none of our business, what! See you in Peter's studio, there's a game of bridge on, I think. Ta-ta."

Meanwhile Edward Povey was walking up Clay Hill in a ferment of thought. It seemed ten years rather than one week since he had been on his stool in the dingy Eastcheap counting-house. He had hoped for a little excitement to enter into his life, and he was getting excitement to the full. He had not looked upon the borrowing of Adderbury Cottage as a crime; the advent of Uncle Jasper and Aunt Eliza was nothing more than a farce—but now tragedy was playing a hand in the game in the shape of a Parisian murder.

He stopped suddenly as a thought struck him. It could not be long before Mr. Kyser's business friends heard of his death, when visits would be paid to his houses, to Grosvenor Square and to Adderbury Cottage. It was easy enough quietly to leave the place himself and to take Charlotte; with Uncle and Aunt it was different. Various schemes entered into his head for effecting their departure, schemes that made poor Edward think that given opportunities he would have made a first-class criminal.

The ruse upon which he finally decided was an inspiration. He laughed to himself as the absurd simplicity of it all came home to him.

He retraced his steps to the village, this time choosing the Red Lion, and engaged a fly to carry him down into Watford, where he entered the same hotel that he had patronized in the morning. He made straight for the writing-room where he remembered having seen some headed note-paper. Then he wrote himself a letter, signing himself Henry Birkett, Public Analyst for the County of Herts. In the letter he said that the sample of water submitted to him from Adderbury Cottage was of a very dangerous description. He said that any one living in the afore-mentioned Adderbury Cottage was running a grave risk. The place, he added, must be in a deplorable sanitary condition, and that steps must be taken at once to overhaul the drainage.

With this missive in his pocket, Edward Povey reached Adderbury Cottage about eight o'clock.

The party were just sitting down to dinner, and were, with the exception of Charlotte, in a genial mood. Mrs. Povey, poor woman, showed plainly the anxiety and strain of the time she had been through, but Uncle Jasper was in fine form. He had already started operations on the garden, and was full of projects for the morrow. Edward smiled grimly as he listened to his talk of roses and cucumbers.

When dinner was over, the two men sat smoking and talking of various things, still mostly gardens. Aunt Eliza had gone to her rearranged bedroom, whilst Charlotte could be heard in the kitchen, to which place the poor woman had flown many times in the course of the day as to a harbour of refuge.

Purposely allowing his pipe to go out, Edward took from his pocket the letter he had written to himself, and tearing off the blank sheet made a spool with which he relit his pipe. Then leaving the rest of the letter on the table, he made some excuse and went from the room. He left the door ajar, and watched the reflection of his uncle in the mirror of the sideboard. In less than three minutes he found that his faith in the inquisitiveness of his uncle had not been misplaced.

Edward Povey tiptoed to the kitchen, and, hastily warning his wife, awaited developments. They were not long in coming.

A chair was thrust hastily back and agitated steps left the dining-room and creaked upstairs. Voices in discussion were heard above. Then Uncle Jasper came down. He was boiling over with wrath as he entered the kitchen, and to Edward, who knew the circumstances, the old man's efforts to disguise his feelings were not without their humour. The old man felt at that moment that he would have given half his fortune to tell the pair before him what he thought of them. But for once in his life Jasper Jarman had met his match. To admit that he had read another man's letter was not to be thought of. Equally impossible was it for his wife and himself to remain another night in the pestilential atmosphere of Adderbury Cottage. He made a gurgling noise in his throat, then:

"I'm sorry, Edward, but I had forgotten this is the 3rd. I have to be in Kidderminster by twelve o'clock to-morrow—I—I—it means thousands to me."

He glared at them in impotent rage for a moment, then went on.

"You must get us a cab, Edward—now. There's only one way, and that is to drive into Watford and stay there and catch the early train to Birmingham in the morning."

"But surely, uncle——" Charlotte began.

"The only way, Charlotte, my dear, I assure you. Edward, there is a cab to be had, I suppose?" The old fellow was clenching and unclenching his hands, his eyes were round with anger.

"If you must, uncle, you must. I know what business is. Charlotte, give me my boots, I'll get a conveyance here in half-an-hour."

Charlotte never could tell how she got through that dreadful half-hour. Uncle Jasper, muffled in his coat, was treading the gravel of the path furiously. Aunt Eliza, her lips a thin thread, was seated on her box in the porch. From time to time they addressed a few words to their hostess, the very forced civility of which was obvious from the way they were jerked out. Then, at last, a rattling old landau appeared, and the last scene of Uncle Jasper's visit to Adderbury Cottage was reached.

As the vehicle rattled away Edward heard the explosion of his uncle's wrath and the restraining *hssh* of Aunt Eliza.

At seven the next morning Edward Povey borrowed a farm cart from an adjacent cottager and sent on their things to Harrow Station. It being a fine morning, they elected to walk.

At ten-thirty the representatives of the late Mr. Sydney Kyser paid a visit to Adderbury Cottage and made an inventory of the contents of that desirable residence.

CHAPTER VI.

AT THE UNION HOTEL, PENZANCE

There was a quietude about the little front dining-room in Belitha Villas that was very soothing to the somewhat strained nervous systems of Mr. and Mrs. Povey. Each in their accustomed positions and chairs they gazed into the small fire that was burning brightly in the grate. Upon the table were the remains of lunch. Charlotte's expression was one of repose, but her husband's brows were contracted as he puffed at his pipe, which was not to be wondered at considering he was turning over in his mind how he was to acquaint Mrs. Povey with his intended departure.

"I am expecting, Charlotte," he began at last, his eyes fixed meditatively upon a hissing jet of gas that was escaping from the coal, "to be leaving the country shortly on business."

Mrs. Povey, who during the last three days had ceased to show or even feel surprise at anything her husband said, merely remarked, "Oh!" dully.

"Yes, my dear, and I want you to shut up the house—I have my reasons—and take rooms at Abbot's Hotel during my absence."

At this the lady became rather sarcastic.

"Or the Ritz, Edward, it seems to me that——"

Mr. Povey held up a silencing hand.

"I don't want to hear what it seems to you, my dear, I want you to go up to Abbot's and take a suite this afternoon. I intend to allow you—er—five pounds a week, Charlotte; I think that should be sufficient."

The surprise that the good lady would not allow herself to show had at least the effect of keeping her silent. Her husband rose and went out into the hall, returning immediately with his hat in his hand.

"I am going out, my dear, and will call back in an hour with a cab. You needn't unpack the things, we'll take them with us."

For fully ten minutes after Edward's departure Charlotte sat in thought before the fire, and then rose to take a look round the house before leaving it. It was strange for this woman to be thus doing the bidding of a man for whom she had hitherto had such scant respect. The change that opportunity had worked in her husband would not have been welcome to her but for the promise of better times that his words and actions suggested. She could not but look forward to the suite at Abbot's, the hotel in Bloomsbury at which they had dined two or three times during their married life.

As she walked slowly from room to room she found herself picturing the glories that were to be hers, the lofty dining-room with its pillars of marble and the windows with the long red curtains. Then her thoughts ran to the five weekly pounds that were to be hers also, and she wondered if Edward meant her to pay for the suite out of them.

She dressed herself in the best that her wardrobe afforded and gathered together a few personal belongings into a small hand-bag, which, together with the trunk and portmanteau they had that morning brought from Bushey, she placed in the hall to await her husband's return. It was four o'clock when Edward softly closed the front door of No. 8, Belitha Villas, and with Charlotte and the luggage clattered away in the decrepit old four-wheeler which he had fetched from the rank.

As they turned the corner, Edward, who had been idly gazing from the window, drew back sharply into the shadows of the vehicle. He signalled the driver to stop, and getting out, walked carefully back to the corner, where, with his eyes, he followed the movements of two men who were looking up at the numbers of the houses. They paused at No. 8, and pushing open the gate marched up to the door. Edward saw one of them knock, then he hurried back to the cab.

"Just in time—I thought so," he muttered.

He then told the cabman to drive to King's Cross station. Arriving there he dismissed him, and taking another cab deposited his silent but wondering wife at the door of Abbot's Hotel.

Then, after booking the suite of rooms, he left her, and entering a passing taxi was driven to St. Mary Axe.

*****

A few days following the hurried and undignified evacuation of No. 8, Belitha Villas, a smart and exceedingly well-groomed little man was contentedly sitting in a front private room of the Union Hotel at Penzance.

The intervening days had been very busy ones indeed for Mr. Edward Povey, and ever since the Cornish Riviera train had set him down on the shores of Mount's Bay he had considered that a complete rest was due to him. Besides, he told himself that it wanted two days yet till the 15th of November, and until that date he had no need to pay his visit to the heiress to the throne of San Pietro.

He had seen her once driving a smart little governess cart through the quaint and steep streets of the Cornish town, and he had found out her identity from the unsolicited testimony of the aged waiter who had noticed him looking at her.

"There she goes, bless her, the best little woman and the best heart in the Duchy," he had said, crossing the room to the window and letting his eyes follow the dainty little lady as she leant out of her trap to give an order to the grocer who had left his shop and stood rubbing his hands together on the curb. Edward had asked who she was

"That's Miss Baxendale, sir, her who lives out to Tremoor Churchtown; not a man in West Cornwall who doesn't worship the ground she drives over—no, nor a woman either, which is saying a goodish deal. When my wife was down with sciatic, sir, she didn't want for naught, she——"

But Edward was not listening, he was gazing spell-bound at the object of the old man's talk. And a picture she made well worth the regard.

Miss Baxendale had now descended from the "jingle" and was standing chatting to the grocer in his doorway. Edward Povey looked in admiration at the trim little figure clad in its well-made white mackintosh that reached almost to the heels of the tiny brown walking boots. Her face was turned three-quarters towards him, and for the first time he began to doubt his wisdom in entering upon the adventure.

Curiously enough the personality of the Princess had not entered into his calculations, he had looked upon her merely as a unit in the scheme as a whole, a spoke in the wheel of the undertaking.

Now he asked himself what he was to do with this perfect creature, a very queen among girls, a being whose every look and gesture spoke of the highest breeding and culture, a girl in whose presence he could not but feel awkward and ill at ease. He had half an idea then and there of abandoning the whole affair, and going back to London, but second thoughts brought back memories of two deserted houses and pointed out to him that he had gone too far to retreat. It was a momentary return of the Edward Povey of a few weeks ago, of the personality he had striven to put behind him.

He alone of all people knew the history of this lovely girl, and in his possession were the papers and trinkets given him in his final interview with Mr. Nixon, all the evidence which proved the high descent of the Princess. In his hands alone was her future. He remembered, too, the generous balance now standing to the credit of himself, Mr. Sydney, in the Royal Bank of Spain. To this, as he was pleased to read Mr. Baxendale's letter, he felt himself quite entitled, as the one who had undertaken the mission. Before leaving London he had burnt his boats beyond redemption, and to give in now would not only mean a return to the old hated life, but he feared he had laid himself open to criminal proceedings.

Charlotte he had provided for and had left that estimable lady in a state of delighted bewilderment at Abbot's Hotel, and the thought of returning to her, for both their sakes, was distasteful to him in the extreme.

After all, why should he not go on with the matter to which he had put his hand? Although a clerk, Edward Povey was one of those quiet-mannered men who can pass muster anywhere and in any society can hold their own by reason of their ability to efface themselves when necessary. He had been well educated and was possessed of a soft and careful diction. Also he was endowed with the most valuable knack of adapting himself to circumstances.

As he turned from the window he caught the reflection of himself in the large gilt-framed mirror that hung over the mantelpiece, and although he had seen the same reflection but a few minutes previously it now took on a new significance. If anything had been needed to endorse his decision to go on with what he had begun he found it in the picture, for he was confronted with a vastly different aspect of himself to that he had been used to as shown by the little cracked looking-glass in the counting-house of Messrs. Kyser, Schultz & Company in Eastcheap.

He saw a trim, dapper little person, looking not a day older than thirty-eight, with a keen, clean-shaven face that bordered on intellectuality. The gold-rimmed spectacles which framed his mild blue eyes together with his thinning hair gave him even a scholarly aspect. Edward had made good use of his newly acquired cheque-book, and he noted with satisfaction that the dark grey suit he had bought in Jermyn Street fitted him to a nicety. His linen was spotless, and a small black pearl showed with a dull richness in his dark blue tie. A thin gold chain across his waistcoat and a signet ring with a deep claret-coloured stone gave a touch of well-being to his appearance. His glance left the mirror and travelled down to his well-cut trousers, thence to his brown brogued shoes. Yes, he was eminently presentable, and as he turned again to his easy chair and his paper, he laughed at the recent doubts that had assailed him and which now were falling from him like water from the proverbial duck.

It was a local journal of little interest and he read on for some moments listlessly, then with a smothered cry of astonishment he turned the paper more to the light and his listlessness gave place to concentration. There under the heading of London Topics was something which set the blood racing through his veins.

THE   MYSTERIOUS   DEATH   IN   PARIS
REMARKABLE SEQUEL TO THE MURDER OF MR. KYSER THE
MYSTERY OF THE BUSHEY COTTAGE

(Special to the "Evening Post")

"It will be remembered that the Post was the first to report, a few days ago, the mysterious death in Paris of Mr. Sydney Kyser, a partner in the great firm of Spanish Bankers and Merchants of Eastcheap. Our reporter in an interview with Mr. Schultz has discovered that there seems to be far more beneath the mystery than was at first supposed.

"It appears that the deceased gentleman's departure from London was unknown to any one, not excepting Mr. Schultz himself,

and as a meeting between the partners, to go through the scrip of certain Spanish bonds in the possession of the firm, had been fixed for the following day, Mr. Schultz was naturally astonished at the non-appearance of his partner. This astonishment gave place to consternation when it was discovered that the safe containing the bonds, of which only himself and Mr. Kyser knew the lock combination, had been rifled.

"Enquiries at Mr. Kyser's house in Grosvenor Square elicited the fact that the housekeeper in charge was also unaware of her master's absence from England, taking for granted that he was at his cottage at Bushey Heath, a little property at which Mr. Kyser was fond of spending a few days from time to time.

"Mr. Schultz thereupon dispatched two of his trusted clerks to make enquiries. Their report is disquieting in the extreme. Adderbury Cottage had certainly been in occupation since Mr. Kyser's death. This fact was evident from a fire still burning in the grate in the dining-room and from the remains of breakfast upon the table. The only people near were the representatives of Mr. Kyser's solicitors, who had evidently read in the Post of their client›s death. These gentlemen, together with Mr. Schultz›s two clerks, made a thorough search of the cottage. On all hands was evidence that the occupants, whoever they were, had made a very hasty departure.

"A clue, however, was obtained by one of the solicitor's men who made a tour of the near-by cab yards. He elicited the fact that a vehicle had been hastily ordered from one of them on the previous evening, and that the cabman had driven an elderly lady and gentleman to Bushey station. His fares seemed to him to be in a very disturbed state of mind, the gentleman especially so. The cabman thought that they were man and wife because he swore so.

"This couple leaving so hurriedly on the evening on which Mr. Kyser's death was reported in the Post is, to say the least of it, suspicious, and they have been traced to some extent. They took first-class tickets for Euston, travelling by the 9.49 train. In London all trace was lost of them, but a porter states that they were seen again early the next morning entering the 7.10 for Birmingham. Here the scent is lost for the present, though from the minute descriptions furnished by the different railway officials and the cabman of Bushey, the suspected man bears a great resemblance to a well-known manufacturer in the

Midlands. *It seems, however, absurd to identify this prosperous and much-respected man with Mr. Kyser and his affairs.*

"Another matter which causes some speculation is the fact that the caretaker of Messrs. Kyser, Schultz & Company's offices asserts that he saw his master in company with a clerk who had that day been dismissed, enter a grill-room in Gracechurch Street. The two representatives of the firm after leaving Bushey called at this clerk's address in Clapham, only to find that this house, too, had evidently been hastily vacated in much the same manner as Adderbury Cottage.

"There, for the present, the mystery rests. The police, who have been communicated with, are, in the mean time, doing their utmost to trace the elderly gentleman and lady who took the train to Birmingham."

Mr. Povey put down the paper and whistled softly to himself. Then as he thought of poor Uncle Jasper and Aunt Eliza, the mirthful side of the affair took him and he laughed for ten minutes.

He rang the bell and told the waiter that he thought he would take a Scotch whisky and a small Apollinaris.

CHAPTER VII.

TREMOOR

The morning of November the fifteenth dawned full of promise. For three days previously the toe of Cornwall had been victimized by sea-mists, accompanied by a lashing rain from the south-west, and the time had hung heavily upon the hands of Mr. Povey. He appreciated now to the full how he had cut himself adrift from his whole past, and the knowledge that even his address was known to no living soul gave him a curious and chilling sense of isolation.

He took moody walks about the straggling town or along the deserted promenade to the fishy but artistic Newlyn, where he would stroll aimlessly through the steep and narrow streets or stand and gaze out over the froth-capped waves of the bay to where St. Michael's Mount rose a gaunt, grey silhouette in the prevailing gloom. The evenings he spent in the cosy little bar at the back of the hotel.

The papers, which he devoured greedily, were silent on the Kyser mystery, and Edward could only speculate on the way things were going, and he smiled as he wondered if they had arrested Uncle Jasper yet.

He had written a long and comprehensive letter to the Princess, acquainting her with all the facts of her birth and the tragedy which had followed it, and of his mission. It had seemed to him a far easier course than telling her all the details personally. He referred her to her nurse for all particulars, and he told her that it was in deference to Mr. Baxendale's wish that he was deferring the pleasure of calling upon her until the actual day of her birthday.

Edward admitted to himself that there was a suggestion of nervousness in his manner as he made a more than usually studied toilet. He took simplicity and dignity as the keynotes of his attire, choosing a black cravat and black *suède* gloves as a mark of respect for the tragedy in the case. This he looked upon as an inspiration and one calculated to make a good impression upon the Princess. His brown shoes, too, he discarded for a serviceable pair of black walking boots, it being his intention to walk the three or four miles to Tremoor. He stopped at a florist's and purchased a little bouquet of white roses.

The promise of the early morning had been duly fulfilled, and the sun shone a glorious augury on the undertaking, as at ten-thirty he left the hotel.

The road he took was one to the north-west, and, after leaving the town behind, it led him into a treeless, desolated district of wild moors and granite-strewn carns. Villages of a few houses, scattered here and there, showed white-washed walls and grey lichen-patched roofs against the golden glory of the bracken. Across the moor broken stone hedges straggled out at odd angles, and buildings falling into decay, roofless and with floorings of rank vegetation, spoke of the time when this district was populated by men engaged in wresting the wealth of tin from its fastnesses in Mother Earth. A cluster of dead mine buildings showed gauntly upon the horizon, their tall chimneys and ruined engine-houses crumbling into decay—a very Pompeii of Industry. From the high ground the sea could be seen on two sides— facing him to the north the Atlantic, whilst to the south the waters of Mount's Bay reflected the blue of the cloudless sky.

Tremoor Churchtown lay in a valley between two rugged carns, a valley which, if followed, would lead to some rocky cove whose silver-sanded beach gave upon the broad Atlantic. As Edward topped the rise and stood looking down upon the peaceful hamlet with its square church tower, he asked himself whether Baxendale had been wise to wish to destroy the bliss of the Princess's ignorance—whether it had not been better that she should know nothing of the stress of power, but that she should spend her life doing good to those in the little village at his feet.

Then Edward Povey shook himself, and with a firm tread picked his way between the gorse bushes and the ivy-covered boulders down to a trim little house that stood at the edge of the cluster of white-washed cottages that comprised the village of Tremoor.

As he paused at the little green gate let in the rough stone wall, the door opened and the Princess came smilingly down the path to meet him. She walked with the springy step of youth and health, and held out her hand with an engaging frankness.

A little below the medium height, the Princess made up in dignity what she lacked in inches. Never had Edward seen such a perfectly proportioned little figure, nor such a graceful carriage. She was dressed in a tailor-made gown of dark blue cloth, and in her chestnut hair she had threaded a black ribbon.

Her face was rather round than oval and the chin was dimpled. The mouth, too, when she smiled caused other dimples to leap into play, and one could easily imagine that she very often *did* smile. The eyes, large and dark, laughed and danced beneath a pair of perfectly drawn brows, fairly thick and arching, and tapering down to a point that looked like a single hair at their ends. Her cheeks, tanned a delicious brown by the Cornish sun, were a little flushed with excitement.

"Mr. Sydney, is it not?"

Edward bowed and raised his hat.

"And you are the Princess Miranda," he said.

The girl put a finger to her smiling lips.

"Not that here, Mr. Sydney—here, in Tremoor, I am Miss Galva Baxendale—my friends would not know me by any name but that."

She turned as she spoke and preceded him up the little path, bordered by clumps of hydrangea, veronica and fuchsia, to the house. The garden on either side of the shingle path, a curious mixture of vegetables and flowers, glowed with all the tints of autumn.

At the door of the house a lady was awaiting them, a white-haired woman of some fifty years of age, tall, and with the most piercing black eyes Edward had ever seen. She received him graciously, and led the way into a room to the right of the little passage. It was an apartment larger than one would have looked for in a house of the size, and was low-ceilinged and lighted by two diamond-paned windows which looked over the moor.

The walls, papered a dull grey-green, were wainscoted to the height of an elbow with dark oak, and were hung with etchings and engravings, mostly of local scenery, in narrow black frames. The table laid for luncheon was tastefully decorated with little silver pots containing slender ferns, and in the centre a tall glass held a sheaf of late campions.

Edward felt at ease immediately with his two hostesses, and he appreciated to the full the well-served meal. The subject of the "mission" of Mr. Sydney was not touched upon until coffee had been brought, then—

"And what is it you are going to do with me, Mr. Sydney?" the girl laughed across the table.

"I—I hardly know, Miss Baxendale; the matter rests more with you, I think, than with me. I'm merely here if I'm wanted, as it were." He turned to the elder lady. "There is, I suppose, no two questions on the matter—I mean on the matter of our journey?"

For a moment there was silence between the three. When Miranda spoke, a suggestion of sadness had come into her voice. She rose and put her arms round her foster-mother's neck.

"*You* want to go to San Pietro, Anna,» she said, «for all these years you have been away from your native land. There must be many things that you pine for over there, many friends you will want to see."

Anna Paluda raised her fine eyes to the girl's face.

"Yes, Galva, my dear, there are many things I want to see."

She spoke sadly, and Edward turned in his chair and gazed out over the wild waste of heath aglow with its tints of cinnamon and mauve. A kestrel wheeled slowly across his vision uttering its dismal cry.

His thoughts were of the sad-voiced, white-haired lady—and again a unit in the adventure took individuality.

For the first time he thought of what the enterprise meant for Anna Paluda. Away in the vaulted splendour of the cathedral at Corbo, her baby had been sleeping unavenged for fifteen years, sleeping on a royal breast in a tomb emblazoned with the arms of the Estratos. What had been the anguish of this mother's heart, who, for the sake of her secret, had been forced to nurse her grief alone? What a cruel scourging of the old wound the return would mean to her.

When Edward turned again, Galva had resumed her seat. He drew up to the table and took from his pocket the things that Mr.

Nixon had given him, a few articles of jewellery, and a letter. The girl opened the letter. It was addressed to

SEÑOR LUAZO,
Calle Mendaro, 66,
Corbo,

and set out at full length the history of Mr. Baxendale's find in the wood. Not an item of evidence had been overlooked that could prove the truth of Miranda's parentage. The jewellery comprised two or three rings and a brooch, engraved with the royal arms. These Anna had snatched up in their hurried flight from the palace.

The princess read to the end, but there was nothing that she had not already learnt from her foster-mother. On the arrival of Edward's letter, two days previous, Anna had told her charge the whole history. To her mind, the evidence was not as complete as she might have wished. She tried to look at it with the eyes of strangers, to whom the story of the substitution of the children might suggest a plot.

They discussed the matter in all its bearings. The love of adventure and the call of romance appealed strongly to the eighteen-year-old girl, and made the suggested journey a very desirable thing. They would go to Señor Luazo in the Calle Mendaro, and place the whole facts of the affair before him. There could be no harm in that. They would travel under the names of Mr. Sydney and Miss Baxendale, his ward, and, with the money at their disposal, could stay in Corbo and see how the land lay. There would be nothing in their appearance or manner to single them out from the other families who wintered in the little white villas that bordered the beautiful bay of Lucana, which was fast rivalling Monte Carlo as a pleasure resort. The names Galva and Baxendale would suggest nothing. The girl had dropped her real name of Miranda for so long; she could do so for a few months more.

The cottage in Cornwall need not be given up; some woman in the village could easily be found to look after it during their absence. In the mean time, Mr. Sydney (as Edward must now be called) must bring his traps from Penzance and stay with them at Morna Cottage.

*****

It was late afternoon, and the two women were taking a last walk on the carn above the house in which they had lived so long. The scene around them was magnificent in the extreme. Away to the west sea and sky were stained with the afterglow of the setting sun. Around them the desolate moors stretched out in gentle undulations, shadowy and mysterious. In the clear twilight the lights of the coast shone out; below them, the four flashes of Pendeen, and, further up the shore, Godrevy and Trevose flickered uncertainly to the distant sight. In a little while it would be dark enough to make out the light on the Scilly Islands, blinking like a great red eye over the Atlantic.

The village in the valley was fast merging into the dusk; here and there a yellow light twinkled from a window. Miranda grew sad as she looked.

"It is all so beautiful, Anna, and I have been so happy here. I fear sometimes at the journey we are taking—perhaps we will never see all this again, and I love every stone of Tremoor."

Anna Paluda placed her arm tenderly round the young shoulders.

"There are fine sights, too, in San Pietro, Miranda—*our* land. I can remember now the colours that the Yeldo hills take in the evening; the sea, too, is beautiful in the bay, and we also have the storms that you love to watch so much.

"Besides," she went on, "you may return, but I—never. I, too, had a 'mission'; it is nearly over now, and I must stay with my child. No—don't pity me, Miranda; the time of tears is long past, but the grief is here still. But we won't talk of my mission. This is not the time for troubling your royal little head over the long-ago affairs of an old woman."

With arms linked affectionately they walked down to the house.

CHAPTER VIII.

THE PANIC OF A CARPET MANUFACTURER

In the spacious library of Mr. Jasper Jarman's house, "Holmstrand," in a respectable suburb of Kidderminster, the wealthy carpet manufacturer was sitting at his ease. On a tiny table drawn up to the fire stood a silver coffee service and a small decanter of brandy. Across his knee lay the unopened copy of the *Midland Echo* which had just been delivered.

Indifferently he took it up and turned to the market reports, reading the comments from the London correspondent through carefully. Then he read half a report of a divorce case, then—he read the paragraph that had caused his nephew by marriage to laugh for ten minutes in the Union Hotel at Penzance.

But the news that the flower of Scotland Yard were following up with a keen interest the movements of himself, Jasper Jarman, and his wife since their eventful departure from Adderbury Cottage was not calculated to draw a like explosion of mirth from the elderly gentleman taking his after-dinner ease in his library at "Holmstrand." Perhaps Mr. Jasper Jarman was deficient in his sense of humour.

He skimmed through the account hurriedly, then starting up from his leather arm-chair he walked to the door and turned the key. For some reason for which he would have found it difficult to account he walked on tiptoe. Then he took the paper, and standing under the cluster of electric bulbs that hung from the centre of the ceiling, he read the report again, carefully this time, assimilating every point.

Then he put the *Midland Echo* on the fire and watched it crumble away into ashes, continuing to stand there upon the hearthrug deep in thought.

There were many aspects of the position in which he found himself that he alone could see. At first it seemed best to him that he should go to the police and explain to them fully the part he had taken in the affair. But then it was hardly creditable for him to associate himself in so scandalous a matter or to admit such a person as Edward Povey, who to his mind was clearly a guilty person, as a relative. Besides, his story might not be believed.

Inspector Melton, too, would make it as hot as he could for him. He was not likely to forget that Councillor Jarman had voted against the proposed increase of salary for the hard-worked police official. He grew cold and hot by turns, too, as he thought of the handle he was giving to his opponent in the forthcoming parliamentary election, in which he, Jasper Jarman, had been persuaded to stand in the interests of Free Trade.

He remembered with a pang the affair of a fire which had taken place at his warehouse a year since. The insurance company involved had been introduced to him by his nephew, and had been curiously unenthusiastic in settling his claim.

To be mixed up in any police court affair with Povey would be to open the question again. The company had been hard hit and had refused to renew his policy, and Jasper felt sure they would not let pass any chance to get even with him.

There were also some things in the past life of the carpet manufacturer which caused him to shun any chance of cross-examination. There was a man who had invented a new shuttle (a machine from which Jasper had made thousands), who was now living in poverty in the slums of Kidderminster, swearing revenge against the man who had sucked his brain and reaped the reward of his labours.

The more he thought, the more a blind and unreasoning panic seized the soul of the carpet manufacturer. Any connection with Povey would cause much dirty water to be stirred up. Better far, he told himself, to leave the country until the affair had blown over or had been satisfactorily explained. He would have it given out that his health had broken down.

He took an "ABC Guide" from the top of a revolving bookcase and opened it at random: Draycot (Derby)—Draycot (Somerset)—

Drayton (Norfolk)—147-½ miles from King's Cross—Population 486—Ah! that ought to suit in the mean time. He moved cautiously to the door. For a moment he stood in an attitude of listening, then unlocked it. The whole framework of nerve which had made Jasper Jarman what he was, seemed to break and crumble away before the panic which had seized him.

On second thoughts, however, perhaps it were better to bury himself in the heart of London, in the network of the metropolis where it is so easy to lie hidden. He wrote a letter to his wife, who was spending a few days in Birmingham, telling her the fiction of his health, then he rang the bell for the servant.

As the man entered the room and stood awaiting his orders, his master scanned him narrowly. The man seemed quite normal.

Jasper, controlling his voice with an effort, ordered the car to be brought round for him in a quarter of an hour, and after the man had left the room, he took a bunch of keys, and, selecting one, opened a drawer in his bureau. From it he took a small fortune in notes and gold, and going to his bedroom he changed his evening clothes for a blue serge suit and put on a heavy travelling ulster. As he made his way down-stairs he heard the throbbing of the engine at the door.

At half-past eight that evening Jasper Jarman slid out of Kidderminster in his Napier car, and in a wonderfully short space of time pulled up at the Warwick Arms Hotel at Warwick. Here he dismissed the car, and after a light supper took train to London.

From a paper he bought at Euston he learnt nothing further relating to his case, but after a day or two spent in London, he read the tidings that his identity had been established, and that an officer who had been dispatched to interview him, not finding him at his house, had applied for a warrant for his apprehension.

On the shattered brain of the poor man this news had a terrible effect. He saw at once that his flight would be looked upon as a sign of his guilt, and he racked his brain for the name of some country where the laws of extradition were lax. The Argentine rose to his mind, but he had no idea of going so far from England unless it were absolutely necessary. He preferred somewhere where the living would be

more or less civilized and where he could be handy for return when circumstances permitted.

Spain he had heard of, but that was some time ago and there might be new laws now. Then the fate that has the moving of the pieces in life's chessboard whispered in his ear—San Pietro.

Even at this late hour he told himself that it were better for him to face the music, but the good common sense of Stone-wall Jarman was in a state of complete disorganization, and to his panic-distorted brain flight seemed the only thing possible.

His wife would be interrogated, but he was convinced that the machinery of the law could not touch her. For himself, on the other hand, there was a definite issue: if he returned it would be undoubtedly to stand his trial, and he knew what that meant even if he was acquitted, which he was not at all sure would be the case. In any event he said he would be ruined beyond redemption, and his reputation would become the legitimate sport of his many enemies, political and social, in Kidderminster. The fact would remain that he, Jasper Jarman, had stood in the dock beside a man like Povey, who had claimed him as a relative! Far rather would he spend the rest of his days in exile; it would mean leaving the country in any case, and by doing it now he would escape the ordeal that he feared. "DO IT NOW"—that's what was on a little printed card in his office—and he had made it his motto.

Again, how could he hope to explain his hurried and agitated flight from Adderbury Cottage, taking place as it did immediately after the publication in the *Evening News* of Kyser›s death? People would never believe the evidence of the bad drainage if Povey liked to deny it—as he doubtless would. Edward Povey to Jasper›s mind was a guilty man, and he attributed to him all the motives and actions of the most hardened of criminals; he would only be too glad to whitewash himself at the expense of his uncle.

The morning after Mr. Jarman's arrival in London, he had called on his bank and drawn a considerable sum of money in cash. It was not without fear and trepidation that he had done this, but he had told himself that it was then or never, and the hue and cry had not really begun. The manager had met him, and there was no suspicion in his manner. This important point settled, Jasper Jarman had made all haste to shake the dust of his native country from the soles of his "sensible shape" boots.

It was a dull, dripping evening when the carpet manufacturer stood on Paddington platform, waiting for the through express for Cardiff. He was rather a different man to the Jasper Jarman who had only a few nights previously been reading in his library at "Holmstrand." He had shaved off his moustache and side-whiskers, and his iron-grey hair he had attempted to dye black, in which endeavour he had been successful—in patches—and to hide this piebald appearance he had taken to a larger brimmed soft hat. He was buttoned up to the chin in his heavy ulster, and a muffler covered his mouth. He looked for all the world what he was—a disguised man. Had there been a detective watching for him on that train—which there was not—Jasper would have been the first man to merit his attention. His manner, too, was furtive and full of suspicion as he glanced from under the brim of his hat at each passer-by.

He had the carriage to himself, and he gave a sigh of relief as the train slid out of the station on its non-stop run to the western seaport.

With an excess of cunning he disposed of his broad-brimmed hat, by dropping it out of the window as the train crawled through the Severn Tunnel, replacing it with a cloth travelling hat, which he took from his bag.

It was past eleven when he arrived, and the hotel clerk looked curiously at the figure in the ulster who asked for a room. Remembering the looks which the Paddington passengers had given him, he resolved upon a further modification in his attire, and the man who for the next few days lounged about the Bute Dock on the look-out for an unassuming-looking boat to take him as near San Pietro as possible was by no means such a conspicuous figure.

He was successful, after many days, in bribing a passage to Bilbao on a tramp steamer that was about to leave, and without loss of time Jasper transferred his portmanteau, his ulster, and himself on board.

*****

And so it came about that at the same time that Edward Povey Sydney was travelling in luxury with his two lady companions between Calais and Paris (which latter city had been decided upon as the first stopping-place in their journey), his unfortunate relative by marriage was passing the great red light on the Scilly Isles in a rousing south-wester, a gale which sported with the poor little *Bella* as with a cork.

Thus does necessity play games with the best of us, even with Jasper Jarman, who, poor fellow, could not cross the straits of Dover without the most acute bodily suffering.

CHAPTER IX.

DUCAL ATTENTIONS

The Duc Armand de Choleaux Lasuer opened one eye and then the other. Then he shut them quickly and called for his *valet de chambre*, whom he cursed roundly for not seeing that there was a gap between the silken curtains of his bedroom window, a little space of which the winter sun had taken full advantage.

His grace yawned and smothered an exclamation. Then he watched with a lazy interest the sedate and black-garbed figure of his servant as he went about his duties. The brows of the duke were contracted as though in pain, which was not to be wondered at considering the time at which his grace had gone to bed. To be precise, the duke had a shocking head.

"Rémy."

"Yes, your grace."

"What o'clock is it?"

"A quarter to one, your grace."

"Then bring my letters and chocolate at a quarter past, Rémy."

Left to himself, the nobleman turned his pillow over and rested his aching head on the cool freshness and slept fitfully, until Rémy woke him and placed a little table containing a silver chocolate service by his elbow. He then pulled up the blinds, lit the fire, and entered the adjacent room to prepare his master's bath.

Duke Armand tumbled out of bed and thrust his feet into a pair of Turkish slippers and himself into a Japanese dressing-gown, and drew up a commodious arm-chair to the fire. Rémy, hearing the movement, followed noiselessly with the chocolate, beside which he now placed an ivory box of cigarettes and a spirit-lamp.

It was one of Rémy's duties, previous to brushing and folding his master's evening clothes each night, to empty the pockets *en masse* into a small drawer in the dressing-table. The duke was thereby enabled to piece together, by the evidence of the articles, the hazy threads of the previous evening's doings. He now drew out this drawer and emptied the assorted collection in the lap of his barbaric dressing-gown.

A bunch of keys, a menu from Maxim's on the margin of which were pencilled two ladies' names—some loose gold and silver—a pair of white kid gloves torn to ribbons, and a little gold-chain lady's bag. This latter he held up and tried to think how it came into his possession.

All the time that he was in Rémy's hands he thought and thought, but to no purpose. He had a hazy kind of recollection of having seen it before, that was all. It contained a little lace handkerchief and a twenty-franc gold piece, but no initial or other mark of identification could be found.

When his toilet was complete, the young Duc de Choleaux Lasuer stood before the cheval glass in his room whilst he sprinkled a suspicion of Jockey Club upon his handkerchief.

He saw the reflection of a well set up, clean-limbed man of twenty-five, with crisp hair of a dark brown, almost black, curling back from an intellectual brow. The skin was of that olive tint that sets off dark eyes so well.

The duke was dressed in a grey lounge suit with a waistcoat of some dark material sprigged with tiny violet flowers. His cravat, tied in the latest mode, was held in position by a pin surmounted by a large blood-red ruby. The hands were rather large, but with tapering fingers; the feet, in their patent leather boots with *suède* cloth uppers, were long and thin. An aristocrat every inch of him, and a dandy withal, but yet with a suggested air of strength and manliness. In short, his Grace the Duc de Choleaux Lasuer was a very presentable person indeed. So had thought the Princess Galva when she had caught sight of him in the corridors or in the Palm Court of their hotel.

The duke slowly made his way down the wide carpeted staircase, pausing in the foyer to light a cigarette. Then he crossed to the board containing letters and telegrams and glanced idly over them. It was here that he read a notice that any one finding a small gold chain-bag should communicate with the office clerk of the hotel.

In a flash it came to him that he had picked up the dainty little trifle as he went to his room the night before. His friend, the Viscount Mersac, had been with him. What a night it had been, to be sure! The duke smiled at the recollections.

As he approached the office a little man in a dark grey suit and with gold-rimmed spectacles was interviewing the clerk in charge. He turned as the duke approached, and caught sight of the bag in his hand.

"Ah!" he said. "You have found it?"

The clerk looked up. "Your Grace," he said, "this is the gentleman who has advertised. It is his ward who has lost it—the little purse."

It was a trivial incident in itself, yet it was the means of an acquaintance of sorts springing up between the duke and Mr. Edward Sydney, an acquaintance which permitted a whisky and soda together in the buffet and a word or two when they met in the foyer.

The introduction to Galva took place after dinner one night, when Edward was leaving the hotel with the ladies for the opera. The duke's large white motor-car had refused to budge from in front of the entrance, and the girl and her foster-mother had had to walk round it to their waiting fiacre. The duke had apologized very prettily, and Galva's already favourable impression of him suffered nothing from the meeting—rather the reverse.

From that time the young people seemed to be always crossing the foyer at the same time, and once Galva and Edward had accepted the duke's invitation to join him in a spin in the lovely car to Barbizon. It was when he was driving his engine that the duke showed to his best advantage and told clearly that under the dandified exterior was a nerve of iron. To see his capable hands grip the steering-wheel was in itself enough to inspire the utmost confidence.

Galva never forgot that ride and the other rides that followed hard upon it. During her stay in England she had hardly seen a car—the roads round Tremoor were not ideal for the sport, and the novelty of it all was, to her, wonderful. The long, straight, white roads fringed with tall poplars, and the absence of speed-limit, showed her motoring at its best, and she would return to the hotel with cheeks aglow and with fascinating tendrils of hair escaping from the dainty motor-bonnet she had bought in the Magasin du Louvre.

It seemed nearly every day that the great white car sped away from the hotel with the duke at the wheel and the little fur-clad figure of Miss Baxendale tucked up cosily by his side. Edward, who invariably sat with the chauffeur in the tonneau, enjoyed these exhilarating spins as much as any one, but he began to wonder where it would all end, and to ask himself whether he was doing his duty in the sphere to which he had called himself.

He indirectly tackled the girl on the subject one day as they sat after tea in their private drawing-room. Anna was writing in her own room, and the opportunity was too good to be missed. Edward cleared his throat, and started the subject by saying—

"I have been looking out the trains, Galva. We will go through to Madrid, I think. It is a little out of our way, but it will be interesting."

"Why, guardy, you don't want to leave Paris, surely. It's grand here, and old Spain can wait. When I get to San Pietro there'll be a lot of horrid things to think about and to worry us. I love Paris."

"Is it only Paris you are so loath to leave, Galva?"

The princess blushed a delicious pink that did not pass unnoticed by her self-appointed guardian. He rose and straightened himself importantly, pulling down his waistcoat with a tug.

"You seem to take a great delight in the company of the duke," he began.

For a moment a look of resentment came into the girl's eyes, but she rose and put a warm arm round Edward's shoulders.

"Surely you can have no objection to him, guardy. I—I—*do* like him; but I like you, too, and I wouldn›t care to do anything you would not wish me to do."

"My dear child"—Edward was quite paternal—"I think it would be best to see how things are in your country. A duke is a good match for Miss Baxendale—but perhaps not so suitable for the Queen of San Pietro."

Galva made no answer, but stood looking out from one of the long windows at the twilight settling down over the gardens of the Louvre. Edward went on—

"Besides, we know nothing of the duke. Titles on the continent are hardly the same as in England. I don't want to hurt your feelings,

Galva, but the young man keeps shocking hours. I saw him come in at three this morning. I don't think he was quite sober; he insisted on giving champagne to all the hall porters and taking two huge motor lamps to light his way up-stairs."

"Why, guardy! weren't *you* in bed at three?»

Edward gave a little cough.

"Well—it may have been earlier. I—I—had been sitting up reading. I don't sleep very well, Galva. I think it's the change of scene."

The princess turned away so that he should not see her smile.

"I don't expect he's a saint, guardy, but he's most attentive, polite and—nice."

"That's not every thing in a husband, Galva, let alone a consort for a queen. You see, I have to look after your destiny—it's my mission— and I feel we ought to be on our way."

"At once?"

"Well—say the day after to-morrow. Tell the duke if he wants to know your movements that you will be here at this hotel at the same time next year. We ought to be able to manage it by that time, whatever happens. I must ask you not to tell him where we are going. We don't know how the land lies over there at San Pietro, and we don't want any love-sick dukes monkeying round and getting in the way. You don't mind doing as I ask you, do you?"

"My dear guardy, I am in your hands entirely. I wouldn't like to think that I will never see Armand—I mean the Duc de Choleaux Lasuer again, but I'll do as you say, I know you are right, but I—I think he likes me."

"So I think, Galva. Really I have been afraid to be left alone with him for a week past. It would be a nice way to carry out my duty to Mr Baxendale to give you to the first man we meet, even if he is a duke. Besides, if he means anything, he'll wait a year,—don't forget we're dining early, Galva, as we're going to the Porte Saint Martin."

Edward held the door open for her to pass out, then he turned and walked to the fireplace. For some moments he stood, his legs well apart and his back to the fire, communing with himself on his importance.

Then a half smile spread itself over his features as he took his mind back a few weeks to a dejected little bowed figure shuffling its way over London Bridge, and as he glanced round the sumptuous furnishings of the room he now found himself in and compared it to Belitha Villas, the smile broadened out and he rolled on the brocaded sofa in uncontrollable mirth. Then he sat up and drove his fist into a cushion of yellow satin.

"How *dare* I!» he cried to himself, «how *dare* I!—Edward Povey, you›ve made strides with a vengeance from the time when you were a poor little clerk at forty-five bob a week, when you can forbid a queen to marry a duke! Oh, what *would* Charlotte say?»

And the little man composed himself and went to his room to dress for dinner.

*****

In a somewhat secluded corner of the Palm Court two young people were sitting. One of them, a young man of twenty-five was moodily stirring his spoon round and round in a tiny cup of tea. In his other hand he held the fingers of Miss Galva Baxendale.

"A year's a long time," he was saying.

"But you've only known me a few days, and——"

The Duc de Choleaux Lasuer turned to her.

"Nearly a fortnight, Galva, and in knowing you I have known myself. I've been a bit of a 'rotter' as you English call it, but things are going to be different now. I'll turn teetotaler—and learn a trade."

"And get to bed without the aid of two Bleriot lamps?"

The duke drove the spoon through the bottom of the dainty cup.

"Now come, Galva, that's hardly fair; they told me about it in the morning. I didn't know it was the talk of the hotel. You know when it happened?"

"No—why?"

"It was after you had refused to come to the Opera with me, that's when, how, and why it happened."

"In that case I suppose I am an accessory before the fact or something—look, there's Mr. Sydney dressed; we're dining early."

Galva rose.

"You'll not forget to-morrow?"

"No, of course I'll not forget to-morrow, duke—it's our last spin."

Rémy could never understand why it was that the duke was so bad-tempered that night as he dressed him for dinner. But then Rémy was not paid to understand the moods of so exalted a personage as the Duc de Choleaux Lasuer.

CHAPTER X.

THREE HANDS AT POKER

"I remember seeing in a Club I visited last year in Buda, some framed hands of cards—remarkable hands that had occurred in the play there. It is a pretty custom. I have often since wished to start a similar collection. Permit me."

And Señor Gabriel Dasso screwed a monocle into a cold and calculating eye and crossed over to the card table.

"May I take them?—thanks. Most extraordinary. And how much did you win, Lieutenant Mozara, on your four kings?"

The young officer addressed nicked the ash from his cigarette and glanced carelessly over the pile of notes and gold before him.

"Oh, about four hundred crowns—thereabouts," he answered carelessly.

"Then the fair Julie of the *Casino* has a rosy future before her for—shall we say nearly a week?»

At this a laugh came from the Lieutenant's two opponents, and Dasso continued, gathering up the cards as he spoke—

"You're sure, gentlemen, you don't mind. I'll have them framed with a little brass plate with all the particulars. Let me see, Count, you, was it not, who held the full house, aces high too—and you, Captain Olalla, the flush—am I right?"

He went over to where a handsome inlaid writing table stood near the window and returned with three envelopes. The players watched idly whilst he put five cards into each; afterwards placing the three in a larger envelope, which latter he stuck down. Then, taking a tiny fountain pen from the pocket of his white vest, he wrote:—

Three hands at Poker, held by Count Petola, Captain Olalla, and Lieutenant Mozara — Friday the fifteenth of January 1908.

"Many thanks, gentlemen, and a thousand apologies for interrupting your game."

Señor Dasso returned to his position by the fire, one arm resting on the high mantleboard and letting his monocle fall with a little tinkle against his shirt front. The men at the table tore open another pack of cards and resumed their game.

But it was late, and the play became desultory. Following such an exciting hand, the cards ran badly, and after the next "jackpot" the Count and Captain Olalla took their leave.

Lieutenant Mozara carried his glass over and joined Dasso, who still maintained his position by the fireplace. He made way for the younger man, and—

"A good evening's play, eh, Mozara?"

"So so, but I say, Dasso, was it hardly playing the game to drag Julie into it? I don't like being laughed at."

"Oh, a little chaff is the least one has to pay for one's gallantries."

"I expect you did the same, at my age."

Señor Dasso turned and contemplated his handsome face with its iron-grey imperial in the pier-glass before replying.

"Worse, my dear boy, far worse. San Pietro was not then what it is now, but Paris was—Paris—and so was Vienna."

There was silence for a moment, and it was Mozara who first broke it.

"Rather childish isn't it—to keep those cards? They weren't so wonderful, after all; you'll see better at the Club almost any night."

"Possibly—but not so *interesting*."

Something in the elder man's voice made the other look up sharply. His eyes narrowed in his head.

"What do you mean, Dasso—more interesting?"

For answer, Señor Dasso drew up a little table in front of the fire, and taking the envelope from his pocket, handed his fountain pen to the Lieutenant.

"I don't understand this, Señor."

"It means, my dear lieutenant, that the record I have written is not yet complete. You will finish it to my dictation."

"If this is a joke, Señor——"

"Pardon me, it is no joke. You will write at my dictation."

"I'm damned if I will—you forget, Señor Dasso, that you——"

"I forget nothing. I know that I am a guest in your uncle's house. Señor Luazo is the soul of honour, and his sister's child should—but never mind. Again I say you will write at my dictation—or you will blow out your brains here and now—Oh, no, you don't."

For with a snarling sound the young man had made a dash at the packet, but before it could reach the flames a hand closed like steel over his wrist.

"You understand me now—eh?"

"Yes, damn you, I understand that you, a guest of my uncle's, dares to spy upon me. I understand that."

"Is there, then, so little difference between a spy and—a cheat?"

Lieutenant Mozara sank into a chair and covered his face with his hands for a moment, then he reached out for the pen.

"What is it you want me to write?"

The other thought for a moment, drumming his fingers upon the polished surface of the little table. "How does it end—yes—'on the fifteenth of January 1908,› now add—›The hands were dealt by me, Gaspar Mozara. The cards were provided by me—and I won four hundred crowns. God be merciful to me a sinner.'"

With an oath the young man rose, throwing over the table in his agitation.

"I'll see you in he——"

He stopped and gave a little cry as he saw the shining barrel of a small revolver pointed at him.

"You—you would murder me, then?"

"Morally, yes, but not physically unless you drive me to it. I would say you shot yourself at being found out. This," and he tapped the little package, "would prove everything; marked cards are the finest of evidence."

Then the boy—he was hardly more—was on his knees. "Why are you doing this, Señor Dasso?" he pleaded. "Before God it's the first time. You knew my mother—I've never harmed you. I will return the money to-morrow. I—I—wanted it for Julie."

"Yes, I know that, bless her. It isn't the first time that a woman has played my game for me. There is no mercy in ambition, and *I want you*. I can make use of you. Oh, your secret is safe with me, provided you write as I say."

"And place my honour and my life in your hands for ever."

"Precisely, that is all I want."

Tremblingly the boy looked past the muzzle to the steady hand and up to the cruel, thin face. Then he righted the table, and whilst Dasso held the package he wrote.

"And your seal," said his tormentor, when the lieutenant had signed his name, and he fetched a stick of black wax from the writing table. Then after Mozara had sealed it with his signet ring, Dasso placed the envelope in his pocket and leant back with a half smile.

"And now, my dear lieutenant, for my motive. Believe me I like you, and I have no personal objection to your method of playing poker. I can be frank with you now that I have this," and he tapped the pocket over the cards.

"You know what they say here in Corbo, that it was I who engineered the affair of fifteen years ago. They even hint that I took an active part in the doings at the palace on that night. Well, they are not far wrong. It was I who did the majority of the work, seeing that my followers faltered at the last moment. I had too much at stake to risk failure. I had worked hard, believing that the choice of the people would fall on me, failing a direct heir. It did; I was made Dictator, and for a few brief weeks I tasted the fruits of power.

"But Spain was stronger than I, and my crime—my political crime—went for nothing. Enrico was placed where I would sit, and now he is at last paying the penalty of his licentious and foolish mode of life. The King is dying."

For a moment the lieutenant was interested in spite of himself.

"But his nephew will——"

Señor Dasso rose and snapped his fingers.

"That for him. What do the people think or even know of him, a man who has hardly been seen by them, a man who hates San Pietro and all in it—including his uncle? I understand he is in Africa shooting lions at this present moment. When he hears of his uncle's death it will be too late."

"But Spain?"

"Spain has her own troubles now, and I have information that a little diplomacy is all that is needed. It is my hour and I will want help—I will want dirty work done. To-night I saw my chance when I noticed that your cards were marked. I took it, as I take all chances."

"What is it you want of me?"

"There will be many things. First I want you to watch and tell me all about these English people, Miss Bax—Baxendale and her Mr. Sydney. I want you to——"

"I will not play the spy in my uncle's house—he has been a father to me—more than a father."

"But you *play*—in your uncle's house—how you play is known only to you and me—so far. It's not much I'm asking of you, but much or little you'll have to do it. They visit here a great deal, and your task will be easy—and I'll help you with Julie. Half-past one; I'll go now—you'll remember."

Gabriel Dasso descended the broad stairway of Señor Luazo's mansion, and was helped into his sable overcoat by the sleepy man-servant at the door. In the courtyard his motor was waiting, but instructing the chauffeur to keep him in sight Dasso turned up the collar of his coat and stepped out briskly.

It was a lovely night, and the Bay of Lucana gleamed silver beneath the moon. The boulevard that terraced above the beach lay white under the cold glare of the arc lamps which threw a delicate tracery of shadow from the acacia trees.

The town of Corbo was built on a cliff, or rather a series of little cliffs that rose in terraces, upon the highest of which stood the royal palace. Under the gay reign of Enrico I, Corbo had prospered exceedingly, and there was but little remaining of the old and quaint town of a decade ago. Modern hotels, rivalling the palace in splendour and far exceeding it in comfort, lined the lower boulevard, and the Casino lying back in its palm gardens had been erected by a syndicate of Russian Jews and had cost a fabulous amount of money.

The lights were still blazing from its myriad windows as Señor Dasso made his way along the broad pavement, followed at a respectful distance by his car. There was a slight wind off-shore and little bursts of melody came to him at intervals, of a popular waltz played by a string band.

For perhaps half-an-hour the man continued to walk up and down, his chin sunk deep in his collar, then he raised his hand and the watching chauffeur slid noiselessly up to him.

Leaving the lighted thoroughfare the car made its way to the eastern end of the town, which lay in darkness. It was here, in a part that still contained some of the buildings of the old town, that Dasso's home lay. It was a large mediæval-looking structure, more of a castle than a house. When first it had been erected it stood alone, but with the growth of the town it had been surrounded, and portions of its grounds taken in till now it had the appearance of a giant being elbowed and crowded out by pigmies.

Before the massive old gateway the car drew up, and at the sound of the brakes the oak doors opened. Señor Dasso passed in between the two footmen, one of whom relieved him of his coat and hat, whilst the other shot home the great bolts behind him.

"I'll want nothing more," he said shortly, and crossing the hall entered a room on the left. On the table stood a decanter and a syphon. He mixed himself a drink, then selecting a key from the bunch on his chain inserted it in the lock of a small but massive safe that was let into the wall by the fireplace. He took from it a portfolio of black leather, and, seating himself near the lights of a branch candelabra, unfastened the little strap.

It contained a varied assortment of papers, and Dasso ran through them hurriedly until he came to a card bearing a photograph. This he held close to the light and scanned narrowly.

He saw an old silver print of a young and beautiful woman in royal robes. Tall, and of a commanding carriage that savoured somewhat of arrogance, the late Queen of San Pietro looked out from the faded picture. For some minutes Señor Dasso gazed at the eyes, looking away now and again as though conjuring up some picture to his mind. Then he spoke murmuringly to himself, his eyes fixed on the portrait he held in his hand.

"I who knew you better than the others—*I who saw you last of all*—can perhaps see more than the others now. Yes, Queen Elene, your eyes have looked at me again to-night—in the flesh"—he laughed shortly—"but I did not flinch, Elene; the nerves of Gabriel Dasso are as firm to-day as they were fifteen years ago."

For a little while longer he looked, a half smile curling his cruel mouth, then he replaced the photograph in the portfolio, putting with it the three poker hands of Lieutenant Mozara, and again locked it in the safe.

Then taking the candelabra, he ascended the wide oak staircase to his chamber.

CHAPTER XI.

THE LIEUTENANT HONOURS GALVA

The residence which Edward Povey Sydney had chosen for his party occupied a central position overlooking the blue waters of the Mediterranean, and embracing a fine view of the Bay of Lucana from the verdure-clad heights of the western arm to the tiny white lighthouse that stood sentinel on the spur of rock to the eastward.

The house itself was modern, having been built five years before Edward's arrival by a Cornhill financier, to whom the extradition laws of San Pietro offered as much inducement as the climate. But at the end of his first year's residence the call of the joys of London proved too strong for the poor man of finance, and the change from the luxury of Venta Villa to the hardships of a cell at Dartmoor had been as unpleasant as it had been swift.

Whatever may have been the failings of the poor gentleman—and doubtless they were many and varied—he had shown a pretty taste in the designing and building of Venta Villa and a wise expenditure of his—or rather other people's—money. The house stood high, having the appearance of being propped up by a series of little lawns and white terraces. The steps leading from the front portico, widening out as they descended, gave upon a square courtyard in which played curiously-carved little fountains. Palms in green tubs lined this pathway of steps, and the banks of the lawns were gay with flowering shrubs.

Miss Baxendale, looking adorable in an old rose, tailor-made gown, that set off the slender lines of her little figure to perfection, stood on the top step debating how and where to spend the hour or so before *déjeuner*.

It was a glorious morning in late January, and the girl's eyes and cheeks glowed with health as she drank in the delicious morning air. Below her the promenade was bright with a happy, well-dressed crowd, the sprinkling of uniforms adding greatly to the gaiety of the scene. Slender victorias and smart dog-carts trotted up and down under the acacias, and shapely motors threaded their noiseless way in and out of the slower traffic, the sun glinting bravely upon their polished brass and silver.

So occupied was the little lady with the novelty and beauty of her surroundings, that she did not at first notice the scarlet and black figure which had detached itself from the crowd of promenaders and now stood trying to attract her attention at the gateway of the lower courtyard. When she did so, she smiled, and waving her long white gloves, ran lightly down to him.

It cannot be said that she was in any way attracted to Lieutenant Gaspar Mozara, in fact, had she asked herself the question, she would have said that she disliked him, but she was gracious to the young soldier from a sense of duty to his uncle, for since presenting Mr. Baxendale's letter to Señor Luazo, the old aristocrat had done everything in his power to make their stay on the island a pleasant one.

As to the true object of their coming to San Pietro, Galva had been willing, as in Paris, to let things in the mean time shape themselves. Señor Luazo also, when put in possession of all the facts, advised caution.

There seemed to her something horrible in the thought of "plotting" in this gay little kingdom. To her the name of "plot" meant bloodshed and hardships, and the world in all its beauty was so new, and seemed so good to her, that she was loath to endanger her newly-acquired paradise. She had even told Edward that she had no immediate desire to be a queen of anywhere, let alone San Pietro— life in the little villa, overlooking the bay, seemed to her far more desirable than existence in the rather ugly royal palace on the hills behind the town—the palace with its long rows of square windows, that reminded her of a workhouse. And in her own heart she was looking forward to the visit to Paris in a year, and her thoughts ran on the Duc de Choleaux Lasuer more often than Mr. Sydney or Anna suspected. She told herself that she did not want to take that journey as a queen, with a crowd of irritating courtiers and maids-of-honour.

"I suppose this is the height of the season, Lieutenant Mozara," she said, indicating the butterfly throng moving round them as they made their way along the boulevard; "how happy and gay they all seem, and what a happy and gay little kingdom you have here—laughter, laughter everywhere."

"Yes, Miss Baxendale, it is the season—we have a long one. We are always happy here; it is only in the height of summer that it is quiet, and then there's nobody here to see it. All these villas are empty then, and everybody who is anybody is in London or Paris. When the king dies, however——"

"Why, is King Enrico very ill?"

"Surely you have heard, Miss Baxendale, that it is only a matter of months, perhaps weeks. There will be trouble then, I'm afraid. You see, the heir-apparent is not popular. It will be the chance for a strong man then."

"But this heir—is he here, in Corbo?"

"Here? he's never here. It's little he troubles about San Pietro. They say he's in Africa now, shooting lions or something silly. The man who keeps his throne warm for him will hardly welcome him when he does come back."

"And who will this man be—this man who keeps his throne warm?"

The young soldier turned and pointed with his cane to where Señor Dasso's house rose, gaunt and forbidding, above the roofs and gables of the old town.

"Dasso, undoubtedly—and with him will rise others. I am a friend of Dasso's," he added meaningly.

"Which means——?"

The lieutenant made an expressive gesture with his shoulders.

"Who knows? A dukedom perhaps"; then, as he looked at her, "I shall have to be looking out for a duchess."

The girl laughed, and gazed out over the sea.

"She will be a lucky woman," she said carelessly.

For a little while the smart figure in its astrakhan tunic and scarlet riding-breeches walked on beside Galva in silence. During the two months of their acquaintance, Lieutenant Mozara had found himself irresistibly attracted by this beautiful girl from England, and the task imposed upon him during the last week by Señor Dasso had been irksome and distasteful in the extreme. Since the eventful night of the marked cards the two men had not met, but Dasso would soon be getting impatient, and Mozara had during the last few days learnt much respecting Miss Baxendale's presence in San Pietro, and he suspected more.

He found himself between two stools, his fear of Dasso and the unbounded ambition that his suspicions of Galva's parentage had roused in him. As the accepted suitor of the girl by his side he would be in a strong position—strong enough, perhaps, to defy his enemy. But he told himself he must speak before her secret was known, it would be impossible after.

These thoughts ran quickly through his brain as they walked along the crowded promenade. Then, impetuous as ever, he bent his head until his lips all but touched a tendril of dark hair that had strayed from under the fascinating toque that Galva wore.

"You think so, really, Miss Baxendale, that she will be a lucky woman. Will *you* be she?»

In a moment the little face became white and set.

"Lieutenant Mozara!"

"Is it so strange, then, that I should have learnt to love you? We of the South do not hesitate to speak where our hearts are concerned. I ask you, is it strange?"

"I—I—don't know how to answer you, lieutenant, I only know that—that——Oh! I didn't expect this."

"Do you dislike me, Miss Baxendale?"

"Dislike—oh no, but I do not love you."

"And you could never do so?"

The girl paused in her walk and faced the young soldier. "This conversation is distasteful to me, Lieutenant Mozara. If you will have an answer, it is that I could never look upon you except as a friend."

A look of anger came into Mozara's narrow eyes.

"That sounds final," he said rather nastily; "there is some one else, then?"

"You have no right to say that," and Galva thought again of a certain nobleman and of delightful rides in the glades of Fontainebleu.

"Pardon me, Miss Baxendale, I have offended you."

"Offended—no, but I am afraid you have put a stop to a very pleasant friendship. These walks will be impossible now, won't they?"

The girl smiled a sad little smile and went on: "I have some shopping to do, lieutenant, and that street up there looks promising. Do you know, a woman can tell a shop miles away."

She held out her hand, and in a moment she was gone, leaving Lieutenant Gaspar Mozara with anger in his heart.

"So it must be the other way, my lady; Gaspar Mozara does not ask twice." He said this between set teeth, and hailing a passing fiacre, gave the direction of Señor Dasso's house in the old town.

*****

Dasso was sitting reading in the oak-panelled library. It was a dignified apartment, low ceilinged and sombre in colouring. The firelight played richly on the dark red hangings and on the pewter which stood on the low bookcases. In shadowy corners stood suits of armour, with here and there a choice bronze statue.

The ex-Dictator put aside the book and rose as the lieutenant was announced, and held out his hand with a show of greeting.

"I have been expecting you," he said.

Gaspar Mozara drew a chair up to face his host, and threw himself into it with an oath. Dasso looked his inquiries.

"Expecting me, have you? It was useless my worrying you, señor, until I had news."

Señor Dasso rose and put his hand on the young man's shoulder.

"Now look here, Gaspar, there's no need for you to be surly. There are times ahead in San Pietro, and you should be honoured to think that I have chosen you to work with me. Oh, I know you are thinking of those cards—they are just my safeguard, nothing more, against treachery. A hand such as I am playing does not allow of throwing away a single trick, of missing a single chance. Work with me, Gaspar, and forget that you ever played poker."

A manservant entered and placed refreshment on the table and noiselessly withdrew.

Dasso poured out Madeira into two thin goblets of Venetian glass and handed one to the young man, who stood looking into the fire, seeing in the glowing coals the disdainful face of Galva Baxendale. He stood up with a clanking of spurs on the polished oak floor and took the glass.

"To Dasso," he said, with a reckless laugh; "To King Gabriel the First."

He drained the goblet, then: "You may burn the cards, Dasso, as I have burned my boats. Heart and soul I am with you, and any work in your cause I will do, for it is my cause, too, now. And the more devilish the work the better I shall like it. My fiacre is outside, Dasso; I will come again this evening. My news can hold till then; I am taking Julie to lunch at Amato's."

CHAPTER XII.

IN THE CATHEDRAL AT CORBO

Shopping was very far from the thoughts of Galva Baxendale as she made her way up the street that ran at right angles to the promenade. Tumultuous thoughts they were, in which the figures of Lieutenant Mozara and the Duc de Choleaux Lasuer played important parts.

She must have walked a considerable distance, for when she glanced at the tiny watch at her wrist she saw that it was eleven o'clock. At the same moment the sonorous chimes of a clock reached her, and glancing up she saw, between the gables of the houses at the end of the street, the white façade of Corbo Cathedral showing brightly in the sunlight.

It had been her first thought on arriving in San Pietro to pay a visit to the tombs of her ill-fated father and mother. Never having known them, she could not be expected to feel a very poignant or present grief, but the sadness of the story made a deep impression, and at times she tried to tell herself that within the storehouse of her memory there was a corner in which a black-bearded man, a-glitter with scarlet and gold, had place. A fancy, doubtless, and one that would have had no existence had she never left her Cornish home. But the knowledge that she had been born in the palace behind the town, helped the illusion, an illusion of a father, and she grappled it to her soul with all the strength of her loving nature.

Edward Sydney had, however, reasoning with the brain of your true conspirator, been firm. There was, to his mind, a grave risk to the living in a too demonstrative reverence for the dead. It is true he had agreed to one visit to the tombs, as ordinary tourists, and Galva gave a little shudder at the recollection.

She had looked through tear-dimmed eyes at the marble effigies of the monarchs, at the stern cameo of her father, and the cold beauty of her mother. In the latter figure the sculptor had with a cunning hand suggested the form of a little child beneath the drapery at the breasts. Galva had listened as in a dream to the little black-robed sacristan, whose duty it was to show the burial-place to visitors, as he had gabbled through the history of the tragedy. He described minutely the attack upon the palace and told of how the king and queen met their deaths. The baby princess Miranda had her share, too, in the history, and it was evident that no suspicion had ever come into the mind of the little sacristan that the body of the princess had not indeed been buried with the mother.

Galva noticed that the narrator carefully avoided mentioning the names of any who had taken part in the attack, and she found it hard to believe that such scenes could have ever taken place in this kingdom of gaiety and pleasure. There would have been a grim humour almost in this listening to the details of her own death when an infant, were the circumstances less pitiful. She had dropped a gold piece into the box for the masses for the dead, which the sacristan noticed, and he looked curiously at this pretty little tourist who gave so generously.

Then, there had been nothing to tell them from the ordinary sight-seers, and it was the only visit that Edward had thought expedient. And now, finding herself alone, she felt an uncontrollable desire to enter the cathedral and pray for a little while. She would not go against her guardian's wish, but would be content to kneel in the great nave and look through the oak screen that divided the mausoleum of the Estratos from the main body of the church.

The cathedral stood on the edge of the old part of the town, and Galva was struck by the difference in her surroundings. Apart from a group of green-veiled American tourists, who, guide-book in hand, were gazing up at the famous rose window over the central porch, she seemed alone with the natives of San Pietro. She looked in astonishment at the poor houses, with their broken roofs, and their windows stuffed with rags and brown paper, at the mean little shops and at the dirtiness and poverty-stricken look of the people. Little dark-eyed urchins, filthy in the extreme, rolled and played in the gutters unchecked by the untidy women who idled and gossiped in the doorways. The men loafing at the street corners were a lazy-looking set of ruffians, and the whole aspect was most depressing.

As Galva ascended the steps of the building between the rows of ragged and crippled beggars who daily congregated there to expose their miseries to the charitably inclined, a conviction came to her that all this hopeless poverty was the real result of the rule of the dissipated old monarch who lay dying up at the Palace. The new town of Corbo with its palatial hotels and wide boulevards was a whited sepulchre, behind which the sores of the true San Pietro festered in hiding.

As she walked slowly up the high-roofed nave she told herself that she was doing wrong to shirk her destiny, and that in the joys of Paris and Corbo she was apt to forget that she was God's anointed, and that these people were hers. The royal blood of the Estratos leaped in her veins as her duty was so plainly shown to her, and she took from her little handbag a rosary—for Galva had been brought up by Anna Paluda in the true Catholic faith—and registered a vow that with the Blessed Virgin's help she would be the salvation of her people, and would act to the utmost in her power in the high position to which she had been called.

She was in an ecstasy as she stood before the oak screen and let the ivory and rosewood beads slip through her little fingers. The sunlight pierced the emblazonry of the window set high above the tombs, and threw a pure orange stream of radiance upon the sculptured image of the babe at the breast, and the girl watching with parted lips took it for an omen.

Then as her sight grew more accustomed to the vague dimness of the cathedral she started and gazed into the gloom at the foot of her mother's sarcophagus. Dimly outlined against the tesselated pavement knelt the black-robed figure of a woman, a woman who, as she watched, rose to her feet and looking round timidly placed a spray of white blossoms full in the orange light.

With compressed lips and a heart bursting with compassion Galva drew back into the shadow of a little chapel as Anna Paluda, walking with bowed head, passed her and left the cathedral.

*****

It had been arranged that Señor Luazo and his nephew should dine that evening at Venta Villa, and Galva looked forward with no little trepidation to re-encountering the amorous lieutenant.

As she entered the drawing-room where Edward and Anna awaited the coming of their guests, the long mirror facing the door and between the two French windows showed her a picture of a radiant girl in a simple robe of a soft clinging blue material and with dark hair coiled turban-wise around a shapely head.

Edward looked up as she entered and smiled his admiration. He was fast growing accustomed to his changed mode of life, and he was beginning to take as a matter of course things which a few months ago he scarcely knew existed.

It was very pleasant to be standing there on the white bearskin rug in front of the fire waiting to extend the hand of welcome to Señor Luazo and Lieutenant Mozara. He smiled to himself grimly as he thought what either of these distinguished personages would think if they could look back a while and see a bowed little figure shuffling across London Bridge.

Seated in a low wicker chair Anna Paluda was watching with folded hands the flickering of the firelight on the Dutch tiles of the hearth. She looked very dignified in her black silk dress—Anna never wore colours—relieved by a touch of Honiton lace at throat and wrists.

The room was small, cosily so. The carpets and curtains were of a rich terra-cotta and the furniture was brocaded in a dull yellow. Delicate china showed richly in the shadowy recesses of a cabinet, and the little cluster of electric bulbs shaded in yellow silk gave a soft light. The two long windows, reaching to the floor, looked like panels of blue-black velvet in which the lights of the yachts anchored in the bay gleamed like diamonds. One could catch a glimpse also of a balcony on which were pots of shrubs and little green painted tables.

Galva was relieved to find that Mozara greeted her as usual. In fact, he was so attentive to her during dinner that she found herself wondering if she had not taken his remarks of the morning too seriously, and whether he had not been in fun half the time.

The dinner, well served and admirably cooked, was a success, and it was about ten o'clock when Mozara made an excuse to leave them, pleading another appointment. Galva had hoped that he wished the episode of the morning to be forgotten, but as she stood by the drawing-room door bidding him "good-night" he touched on the subject.

"Did you find the shop you wanted, Miss Baxendale?"

She felt the colour come to her cheeks, but the soldier was waiting for an answer.

"No, I'm afraid not—it was rather a disappointing morning."

"It was to me," he said; "but we are friends, I hope, Miss Baxendale, eh? Our appointment for to-morrow holds good, I hope?" And Galva had looked serious for a moment, then smiled sunnily in answer.

Once clear of Venta Villa, the lieutenant turned, and the arc lamps showed the cunning ferocity of his sallow face as he shook his fist at the house he had just left.

"*Friends!*" he hissed. "Yes, my work will be easier if we are friends."

Then he hurried on to keep his appointment with Dasso.

*****

After Galva and Anna had retired, Edward sat smoking with his guest in the little library of the villa. He thought it a good opportunity to talk over the state of affairs, and he opened by remarking on the rumours of the king's health that had been rife in Corbo the last few days.

The old gentleman stroked his long white beard meditatively for a moment.

"It cannot be long now," he said at last; "the good God ease his passing. The princess must hold herself in readiness, for at the moment the breath leaves the body of Enrico, Dasso, who has many friends in the army, will hasten to the Palace, and will cause himself to be proclaimed king. I know that, in this, he has a secret understanding with Spain herself. Miranda—I mean Galva—must be there also, Mr. Sydney; the people must choose."

"And what will Spain say to that?"

"Spain, my dear sir, is powerless where an Estrato is concerned. Enrico's nephew even must bow to her claim. Believe me there will be no difficulty; but it is better to be in time and not to allow Dasso to mount the throne at all. It might be harder to dislodge him once there, than we imagine."

The old man paused for a moment and drew his chair nearer to Edward.

"I saw him look at her very hard that evening they met at my house. They say," his voice sank to a whisper, "that Gabriel Dasso's was the hand that struck down the royal victims that night fifteen years ago. It is said that he and one other alone of all the band of conspirators went right through with it. That other, a Señor Orates, shot himself within a week."

"And the people—do they know this?"

Señor Luazo made an expressive gesture with his hands.

"Fifteen years is a long time, Mr. Sydney, and the people of San Pietro have a short memory. There are a few of us old ones, we who knew the king and his queen, who do not forget. We have been unconsciously awaiting this day for fifteen years. I wonder if Dasso saw any likeness when he looked at her? There *is* a likeness, elusive indeed, but at times I see the eyes of Queen Elene as I have seen them look on those she liked. If Dasso saw it too, he will be dangerous. I would like to come to an issue with Gabriel; regicide that he is, he is received everywhere. His crime has never been brought home to him, and in any case is regarded as a political one. It has made my blood boil, señor, to see him at my table."

Long after Señor Luazo had left, Edward sat gazing into the dying fire. The windows of the library looked inland, and by turning his head he could see the row of lights in the Palace windows. He thought of the dying king and of how the affair that looked at first like being a comedy, might at any moment now develop into a tragedy.

CHAPTER XIII.

THE PLOT

The doorway of Gabriel Dasso's house stood open and the gleam of yellow light that cut into the darkness showed old Pieto the groom holding by the bridle a horse that seemed by its steaming hide to have been hard ridden and but newly arrived. Lieutenant Mozaro slackened his steps as he mounted the hill, asking himself what visitor this could be that rode in haste to Dasso at so late an hour.

Remembering the business of his own visit he drew back into the shadow of the stable yard of a little *posada* that stood nearly opposite. It was striking eleven down in the town and the inn had done its business of the day, and, save for a little square of light in an upper storey, was in darkness. Gaspar leant against the gate-post and watched the horse standing with outstretched neck and drooping head, and the form of the groom silhouetted against the glow of the hall. Old Pieto looked now and again, with a show of impatience, within the house, thinking, no doubt, of the interrupted supper awaiting him below stairs.

Perhaps a quarter of an hour passed—it seemed longer to the man waiting in the stable yard—when the booted and spurred figure of a young man came out upon the doorstep. He stood there a moment drawing on his riding-gloves, and turned and spoke to the master of the house who stood behind him, just within the hall. The young rider took the reins from old Pieto and swung himself gracefully into the saddle. He bent down for a final word or two, then brought his horse sharply round and with a dig of the heels set him at the hill that led inland.

Mozaro was about to leave his retreat when he heard the window of the inn open. From his point of vantage in the shadow, he saw a head emerge—a round bullet-shaped head that took the attitude of listening. It remained motionless until the clatter of the horse's hoofs upon the cobbled street died away, then it turned a face full upon the spot where he stood, and Mozaro gave a start as he remembered that he had not put out his cigar. The face was a strange one to him, and he knew that Detti, the host of the Three Lilies, did not entertain many guests. Moreover, it was not the face of a native of San Pietro. A moment the stranger regarded him fixedly, then with a muttering in a language that was certainly not Spanish, but was undoubtedly a curse, the window was slammed shut and the light extinguished.

The lieutenant turned towards the house opposite. Old Pieto had disappeared, but Dasso still stood upon the doorstep looking anxiously along the road towards the town. As Mozaro came out of the shadow he gave a start, then greeted him eagerly. He drew him inside and closed the stout oaken door.

"There has been great news to-night," he said, and led the way to the library.

The two men seated themselves at the table on which was strewn a few official-looking papers.

"Enrico is worse, Gaspar; I have just heard from the Palace that he may go at any time. The doctors wonder at his vitality."

"Threatened men live long."

"Yes, and there's another proverb, I believe, about it being hard to kill a weed—Enrico may laugh at the doctors yet. But," went on Dasso, "we must be in readiness. Miss Baxendale must be secured or silenced."

Lieutenant Mozara looked straight in the elder man's eyes.

"You mean the Princess Miranda, Dasso."

The other looked up quickly.

"Ah, then you have heard?"

"I have heard enough to know that. I have played the spy well," and the sallow face lit up with an evil grin. "I have suspected the facts for two days now."

He drew his chair closer to Dasso's.

"And what is more, they are waiting for the same signal as you are. When the guns at the Palace boom out the death—well—it'll be the devil take the hindmost."

Gabriel Dasso rose and paced nervously up and down the room, biting his moustache. It seemed to him that here was a grave danger, and he cursed the luck that had brought Miranda to life at the time when his plans seemed so prosperous—when success seemed assured. Then a thought occurred to him and he pulled up sharp before the man who was sitting drumming his fingers on the table.

"It seems to me, Gaspar, that you have taken up my cudgels very thoroughly. Your expression when you spoke of her Royal Highness wasn't a very pretty one. You don't like the lady, eh?"

"No, curse her—I don't."

"So. That's how the land lies. That accounts for your keeping your suspicions to yourself for two days. It seems to me," and his voice grew hard, "that Lieutenant Gaspar Mozara has had a fish of his own to fry."

"You can keep your taunts, Gabriel. I neither understand them nor appreciate them. I am with you in this matter, body and soul—does not that suffice?"

"It is everything, my dear boy. We won't quarrel. Hate is a good weapon. I hope you have not put the princess out of temper with you?"

"Miranda and I are the best of *friends*. I thought it better that we should be. We motor together to-morrow morning. Doesn't that suggest anything to you, Gabriel?"

"My dear Gaspar, it suggests so many things that I'm bewildered."

"Will the news of Enrico's relapse reach the town to-night?"

"It's hardly likely—my source of information is a private one."

"I'm calling for the lady at nine. The news mustn't reach Venta Villa before then, or she will be kept in readiness."

For some little time neither of the men spoke, then Dasso leant over and whispered the plot that had occurred to his fertile and evil brain.

"You will call with the car at nine, as arranged. After a spin twice past the villa to allay any suspicion of the girl being long away, you will suggest a run to Alcador. The road is a good one, and you can open out to any speed. About ten miles out you will see—no doubt you know it—a castle, one tower of which shows up from a little forest of pines.

"You will here pretend that something is amiss with the engine. You will descend, and while she is watching you at the bonnet, a man will enter the tonneau from behind. A chloroform pad will do the rest. Pieto and his wife will be at the castle, which belongs to a distant relative of mine, to receive the guest."

"An excellent plan, señor, but what will they say to me?"

"That's only the first half of the plan. You will turn the car and run back to where four miles from here the road winds ledgewise, round the western spur of the Yeldo hills. There is a low stone wall here, and the curves are dangerous. You will stop here and alight, and set the empty car at full speed at this wall. It will give way easily, and the river, which runs at this spot in a series of falls and rapids, will do all that is needed in the way of evidence."

Mozara opened his mouth to speak, but Dasso held up a silencing hand, and went on: "You will then throw over the cloak and hat that the girl was wearing, and walk on to a cottage which you will see a little nearer the town. Here you will be met by a friend of mine who will transfigure you. Immediately afterwards a cart will leave the cottage containing poor Lieutenant Mozara. His arm will be in plaster of Paris, and his clothing will be torn to ribbons and blood-stained. A bandage will be wound around his poor head." Señor Dasso laughed. "His will have been a narrow escape.

"Search will be made and the wrecked car discovered. Sympathy will go out to the friends of the late Miss Baxendale, whose body will be stated to be in one of the deep holes which abound in the River Ardentella. And so for the second time this person's death will be announced."

"And what will you do with her ultimately?"

"In that we must be guided by circumstances. I see no reason why, if the lady be reasonable, she should not in the long run go free, if not—" he shrugged his shoulders—"I would be generous to her in the way of money, and once on the throne I fear nothing. Spain will see to that."

"And what of her friends?"

"I'll find a way to crush that worm Sydney, while as for the woman—I don't know who she is, a paid companion, no doubt—I don't think she counts."

To Mozara the scheme sounded good. He was not at all anxious to play the part of invalid for long, but, as Dasso pointed out, his injuries could turn out less serious than was at first supposed. Again, he did not like losing the car. But it was revenge that smoothed the way for him. He thought of the proud disdain that had shown in Miranda's face that morning, and it was enough.

An hour later old Pieto and a sour-looking woman, who, by the discourtesy he showed her, was presumably his wife, set out in a covered cart and made their way inland. Again, a little later, two men who had spent an hour with Señor Dasso left and took the same road.

CHAPTER XIV.

AT CASA LUZO

Leading out of the town of Corbo, the Alcador road ascends steeply to the Palace Square, where, leaving the royal residence on its left, it winds away over a stretch of desolate brown moorland and cuts its way through the Yeldo Hills at the Quinlon Pass. Once through, the red fluted roofs of Alcador and the yellow belfry of its church lie spread out before one.

And all the way to the hills the road has for its constant companion the blue Ardentella, running first this side and then that. The many bridges where the road crosses the river are quaint old structures, the architecture of which plainly points to their origin being Moorish.

The casual traveller journeying on this road would pass the Casa Luzo without being aware of its existence. At one time the tower showed above the trees, a landmark for miles around, but that was long ago, and, as the stout stonework had crumbled into ruin, so had the forest spread in density, so that there was now little likelihood of the jagged tower that mingled with the tree tops being noted. True, there was a gateway, but there were no gates hanging on its hinges; only two gaunt pillars of stone, their bases hidden in a rank mass of herbage.

Count Ribero, in whose family the castle had been since Alfonso VI reigned over Spain, never visited his ancestral home, the gay young nobleman preferring the little villa on the shore at San Sebastian which had come to him from his mother. Dasso, therefore, by his distant cousin's invitation made free with the place for all purposes without compunction.

At his own expense he had made a few rooms inhabitable, and the hunting parties and carousals which he had held there had been until lately very popular amongst the gilded youth of the San Pietro army.

But of late years Dasso's orgies had been less frequent. Political ambitions had taken up the time of that enterprising gentleman, and the rooms were beginning to show the effects of non-usage. Large patches of damp were making their appearance on walls and ceilings, and the somewhat gaudy hangings and furniture were fast becoming the happy hunting ground of moth.

Old Pieto felt a thrill of superstitious awe as he turned the key in the massive lock. A chill wind pierced him as he threw open the great door and stepped into the gloomy hall. The lantern he carried threw shaking patches of ochre light on the flagged floor, and an army of rats and spiders scampered away at the approach of this intruder in their domains. One great fellow stood his ground, regarding the intruder with beady black eyes in which the rays of the lantern touched little pin points of flame. With a cry old Pieto flung the heavy door-key, and, squeaking, old King Rat disappeared.

A woman with a thin wrinkled face had been peering over the old man's shoulder, and now she followed him timidly into the hall, holding her skirts well above her ankles and looking fearsomely at the desolation around her. On her arm she carried a large basket, which she now set down at the foot of the staircase.

Old Pieto remembered the last occasion when he had been there, some two months ago, when a supper had been organized by Dasso to celebrate the benefit of La Belle Espanzo at the Casino, and as he opened the door of the dining-hall the scene came back to him in full force.

The long oaken table from which the cloth had been half snatched was still littered with the *débris* of the feast. The old manservant knew that he ought to have cleared it away, but it was a long journey from Corbo, and it had been put off. A tall epergne in the centre of the table had been overturned, and flowers, yellow and brittle, were tumbled together with the wrinkled mummies of fruit, and lay in a scattered heap on the oak floor. He remembered how the young bloods had toasted the lovely dancer, drinking champagne from her slipper. The little high-heeled satin drinking vessel still lay on the table, shapeless now and stained with wine. Pieto noticed that a giant spider web stretched from the dainty rosette of the shoe to the back of one of the carved chairs.

The sight of the disarray of wine bottles suggested the cellar to the old man, and, still carrying the lantern, he descended the broken stone steps at the end of the passage, reappearing almost immediately with a couple of tall thin-necked flasks.

He called his wife and bade her make a fire in the open grate, and soon the blaze shone merrily on the tarnished silver and glass on the table and threw weird and flickering shadows into the corners of the dark panelled walls.

The worthy couple, with chairs drawn up to the genial warmth, attacked the bottles gratefully. It was no joke for the master to pack them off to this spot in the dead of night. The journey had been a long and wearisome one, they had had to walk the last quarter of a mile, and it had rained a little as they came through the forest.

But there was work to do and to do quickly. Pieto was content to superintend operations, and he issued orders from his armchair, while Teresa cleared the *débris* from the table. The old fellow, warmed by the wine he had taken, entertained his wife with reminiscences of the feast. He rubbed his skinny hands together as he talked.

"Ah, that was a night, Teresa—the wine flowed like water—the best in the cellars, too. And the beautiful Espanzo—divine!" the old reprobate kissed the grimy tips of his fingers, "blue-black hair, and a mouth like a splash of wine—and—her eyes as she danced!"

The old woman seemed not to hear him, working steadily, piling the broken glass and fruit into the table-cloth and tying up the four corners. Her husband looked shrewdly at her from beneath his shaggy brows and rambled on.

"On the table, too, she danced, all among the wine and the flowers—and me, too. The gentlemen made me, old Pieto, dance with her, and, as we danced, she sang the tune—how did it go?—yes," and the ancient broke out into a wheezing treble of a weird and sensuous melody, ending in a harsh chuckle as his wife left the room, taking her bundle with her.

Candles had been set upright in the sconces and shed a soft light on the handsome old apartment, to which duster and broom soon gave a look of respectability. The old woman paused and surveyed her work.

"And where is she to be put?" she asked the figure by the fire, who, with goblet in hand, had fallen again to his humming.

"Eh—oh," and he pointed to the ceiling. "Above here, I suppose, for the present—the Duchess room. Hurry, Teresa, it'll be daylight soon. Put a fire up there, the room will be damp—ugh!"

"Ah, you can shiver, Pieto. Why don't you work and get warmth into your old blood? Get me a few logs from the outhouse, won't you? I don't like rats."

"Ay, I'll do that for you. Get you upstairs. I'll bring them up."

Pieto relit the lantern, and his shuffling footsteps died away down the stone passage. There was a creak of rusty bolts and a gust of the chill air that comes before the dawn flickered the candles in the dining-room.

Outside, the old man made his way across a paved court-yard, the stones of which were worn and cracked with age, and little blades of tender green showed between the crevices. One side of the yard was colonnaded, and the moonlight cut clear designs of shadow among the lichen-covered pillars. On the other three sides a high stone wall separated the house and yard from the forest. Pieto could see the sharp silhouettes of the tall pine tops against the star-strewn sky. The rain had ceased, and there was a delicious freshness in the air, and the woodland was alive with the tiny noises of the night.

A bat zigzagged before the man's eyes, and he hurried on his errand. He collected an armful of logs from a shed in the corner and hastened back to the fire. He did not forget to pay another visit to the cellar on his way.

By the time Teresa's labours were finished birds were calling to their mates, and the higher branches of the trees were flushed with the dawn. The dining-room showed ghostly as she entered it. Her husband was still before the nearly dead fire, his arms hanging inertly on either side, the finger-tips touching the floor. A broken glass lay at his feet, and the red wine had run into a little pool. The rays of the newly-risen sun struggled through the escutcheoned panes and cast a variegated sheen over all, and a candle which had outlasted its fellows shone with a pale sickly light. Teresa laid a heavy hand on the shoulder of her sleeping lord.

"Pig," she said.

A snore was strangled at its birth, and Pieto sat up, rubbing his eyes.

"I've been asleep," he said, as though the fact were one that called for amazement.

"You've been drunk, you mean. Get out to the yard, man, and to the pump, and go and lie down on the bed up-stairs. A nice thing," she went on, "if our visitor arrives and those who bring her find you like this. I still have work to do."

The old man looked sullen but did not answer. He ran his tongue round his parched mouth and did as he was bid, while his wife, upon whom this unwonted night-work seemed to have little or no effect, busied herself in the kitchen.

It was about mid-day when a cautious tap at the window brought her hastily to the front of the building. Lieutenant Mozara, his face white and drawn, stood leaning against one of the stone pillars that supported the portico.

"Is all ready? Where's Pieto?"

Murmuring some answer, Teresa ran back into the house, and in a moment returned with her husband. He was but half-awake, but at the sight of the lieutenant he pulled himself together. He saluted the officer, and together the two men ran through the belt of woodland which lay between the house and the road.

Gaspar had done his work well. The figure of Galva Baxendale lay stretched out on the little ribbon of grass that ran beside the road. The car stood vibrating beside her, and with an oath Gaspar ran to it and shut off the engine. Then without further delay the men lifted the unconscious girl and made their way back to the house.

The lieutenant waited only long enough to drain the glass of wine Teresa had poured out for him. His hand shook so that the liquor splashed upon the door-stone, and the glass rattled against his teeth as he drank.

It was evident that the old couple had had their instructions, for hardly a word passed between Mozara and them during the whole time. In the rest of the programme Pieto and his wife knew their parts.

When the captive was safely locked away in the room above, they set about making preparations for the meals of the day. Now and again the woman ascended the creaking stairs and listened at the door of the Duchess room. They had been given to understand that the effect of the chloroform would take some few hours to wear off, but dusk fell and still the victim gave no sign. Then night came down on the castle, and in the dining-room the candles were lit and shone on the sallow faces of the two old people who, with ears nervously strained, still waited and listened.

A night bird screamed in the forest behind them, echoing eerily around the still castle.

CHAPTER XV.

EDWARD SHOOTS AN ARROW INTO THE AIR

In a state of the deepest dejection Edward Povey listened to the story. At times during its recital he would raise his head and look at Gaspar Mozara. The lieutenant, when Edward's head was bent again, eyed his hearer narrowly.

He had told his tale well—circumstantially and yet with the feeling that Anna Paluda, who, sitting rigidly in her chair, never once removed her doubting eyes from his face, did not believe a word he was saying. He found it increasingly difficult to marshal his facts under the fire of those steady watching eyes. Hitherto, this grim lady in black had held no importance for him, but now, as he looked at her and felt her presence, she took on a new individuality. To Mozara it seemed as though an unconsidered pawn belonging to an opponent had crept unobserved up the chess-board of his plans and had become suddenly a force to be reckoned with.

The lieutenant was between two stools. He had told his tale, and was now anxious to be gone, but he felt that no sooner did he leave, so surely some piece of evidence, some vital point in the scheme would occur to him as having been left unsaid.

He had made his way to the little villa as soon as the third-rate medical man, whom Dasso had pressed into the plot, had given the lieutenant permission to get up, a sorrowful figure in deep mourning. His right arm was suspended in a sling of black silk and was tightly swathed in surgical bandages. He had sunk in well-simulated exhaustion into the big chintz-covered arm-chair in the drawing-room facing the sea, and had laid an ebony crutch beside him on the carpet. One leg had been carefully stretched out stiffly before him.

Edward, all unsuspecting, had assisted him in his movements and had opened the windows, letting in the bracing breeze that blew up from the bay. Anna Paluda, however, had merely inclined her head. When the lieutenant entered she had felt only a dull anger against the author of her poor Galva's death. It was only as his story progressed that she grew to doubt the truth of what she was listening to. Gaspar had begun with well-acted expressions of sympathy and with carefully considered phrases of self-condemnation. He told them that the blame of the accident had been entirely his in agreeing to Miss Baxendale's demands for increased speed. The road was one on which he had seldom travelled and they had rounded the spur of the hillside before he was aware of their danger. He had applied the brakes and turned the wheel to keep in the middle of the narrow road but the impetus had been too great. There had been a hideous skid as the car crashed almost broadside into the old and crumbling wall.

The lieutenant had remembered no more until he had come to his senses to find that he was being carried along on some kind of rough litter. The pain and the jolting had caused him again to lose consciousness, and when next he awoke he was in his uncle's house.

There had been no questions from his hearers. Anna had sat rigidly as before, and Edward, his head between his hands, rocked himself gently to and fro. From time to time he gave a little moan.

Gaspar had fixed his eyes on the centre of a rose pattern in the carpet, and had resumed his tale in a low, hopeless voice.

"My first thoughts were of Miss Baxendale and of how she had fared. For two days they would tell me nothing except that she was slightly hurt. I only heard yesterday the true state of affairs, how her cloak and hat had been found in the ravine near the Wrecked car. The river, they tell me, is deep here and weed-grown and there are great rocky holes. I——"

The lieutenant had risen with a choking sound in his throat as he recited these details. He leant heavily on his crutch, standing before Anna and Edward.

"This is as painful to me—as to you. I—I—can say no more." He advanced to the little bowed figure before him and held out a hesitating left hand.

"I would like to hear you say one word, sir. This affair will be with me to the day of my death. I am beyond the reach of Miss Baxendale's pardon, but not of yours. You will perhaps be leaving San Pietro and I would like a word to remember and look back on. It would be one spot of brightness in the darkness of my future."

Edward had taken the proffered hand and the lieutenant had bent low over it, pressing it to his lips. Then he turned for the harder task of facing Anna Paluda. But that lady had taken advantage of his back being turned to slip unnoticed away. Gaspar's relief at being spared the leave-taking was mixed with a disquieting feeling of a pending misfortune. He told himself that it would be long before he could forget the eyes of the lady in black.

Painfully, and with dragging step, Mozara left the house and made his way down the path to the boulevard. The fiacre which had been waiting for him was drawn up at the curb, and into it the wounded officer was helped by the driver, who, mounting his box, turned his horse and drove off in the direction of the Old Town.

Edward had sat where his visitor had left him, the prey to the most poignant sorrow and agony of mind. To his own rash and criminal act in personating another man all this tragedy was due. Although he had, at times, told himself that Miranda would not be seated upon a throne without some opposition, he had never imagined that danger threatened the girl herself. She was so beautiful and tender-hearted, so delightfully modern, that the idea of her being the centre of a plot of scheming scoundrels had barely occurred to him. That an accident should have been the cause of her death was a stunning blow to the little man who sat in the sunlit drawing-room, gazing blankly at the wall before him.

He rose at last with a sigh, and passed out through the French windows on to the balcony. Below him rolled the carriages and motors of the fashionable world of Corbo; from the smart café a little up the boulevard came the sound of strings of a gipsy orchestra and the laughter and chatter of the crowd of loungers who were taking their absinthe. Edward told himself that in the whole of San Pietro there was no house afflicted as was Venta Villa. The flowering shrubs on the balcony on which he stood, the gaudy red-striped awning over his head seemed to mock him, and he turned from the gay scene with a little sob. It was then that he saw Anna Paluda. She was sitting in a low wicker chair, and like him had been gazing out upon the boulevard and on to the blue of the bay beyond.

She beckoned Edward to come to her side, and standing there, one hand resting on the little iron railing, he listened while the lady told him of her disbelief in no undecided voice.

Edward's expression changed as he drank in her words, and the hand on the railing tightened its hold till the knuckles showed white patches of skin. The suggestion of doubt on what he had looked upon as an accepted tragedy was acting as balm upon his spirits, and all the hidden power of his brain was responding to the call and demanding action—deeds.

"And you say you watched him?"

"Yes, from this balcony. As he was getting into the cab, the driver who was helping him stumbled a little. I distinctly saw Señor Mozara put out his *right* hand and grasp the back of the hood. I had doubted before in my own mind, but this is certain. The lieutenant›s right arm is as sound as his left, for all his surgical bandages. Again, why should so important a personage as the nephew of Señor Luazo call in the services of an unknown medical man, instead of the family practitioner?"

The lady paused for a moment, then went on fiercely—

"Oh! I can see it all now. Dasso, the cursed regicide, is at the bottom of this. I, who have suspected the man, have watched his friends. I have seen meaning looks, glances pass from evil eye to evil eye. Mr. Sydney—you will understand that I, too, have a quarrel with Dasso. The hand that struck down Queen Elene struck down my child—the baby at whose tomb I, her mother, have to sorrow in secret——"

Edward laid a hand lightly on the weeping woman's shoulder.

"And my sorrow, Anna, my anguish! Have you thought of that, of what it means to me, who have indirectly brought Miranda to this?"

Anna took his hand between both of hers and looked up at him through her tears.

"You have been kindness itself, Mr. Sydney. You had your duty to Mr. Baxendale and you have done it nobly."

The man turned away and thought of Kyser. Anna's trust in his integrity was almost too much for him to bear. Rapidly the little devils of pro and con invaded his conscience. Then and there he registered a silent vow that come what might he would go through with it. There was no turning back now; he would not add cowardice to his crime. If Miranda were still in the land of the living, his would be the hand that would save her and deal vengeance where it was due. He hoped that, if need be, he might die in the doing. He went into his bedroom and took from his trunk a leather writing-case, and from one of its pockets a letter. It had been handed to him as they left the hotel in Paris, and was from the Duc de Choleaux Lasuer. He had laughed as he read it and put it away in his case. Now he read it with all seriousness. It was merely a short note, in which the writer had set down boyishly his admiration for Miss Baxendale. He had heroically demanded that should that lady ever be in trouble, he should be called upon to come to her assistance. A letter addressed under cover to M. de Brea, the manager of the hotel, would always find the duke.

It was a letter breathing the spirit of knight errantry, such a letter as a love-sick boy of twenty would write. And yet, as Edward read the words under the changed conditions, they seemed to hold a deal of truth and manliness. The duke was a high-spirited young man, a little addicted, as Edward had seen, to the vices of his class, but he had liked and admired him in many ways.

There could be no harm, he told himself, in writing to him. Perhaps his grace had already forgotten that he had written such a letter; but Edward rather thought otherwise.

That evening after dinner he took a letter out and posted it himself. The outer envelope was addressed to —

M. de Brea,
Manager,
Ruttez Hotel,
Rue Scribe, Paris;
the inner merely to —

His Grace le Duc de Choleaux Lasuer
(by the courtesy of M. de Brea).

CHAPTER XVI.

THE GENTLEMAN IN THE TWEED SUIT

It was nine o'clock when Mr. Povey left the little modern red-brick post-office situated in one of the principal thoroughfares, that ran steeply inland from the boulevard, and made his way down the hill.

Nine o'clock was an important hour of the twenty-four to the inhabitants of Corbo, for it was then that the late edition of *El Imparcial de Corbo* made its appearance. The editor and proprietor of that enterprising journal had an arrangement by which the latest European news was sent to him direct from a relative employed on the staff of one of the great Parisian papers. There was another paper published in Corbo, but it was not one that appealed to the sensation-loving San Pietrians. *El Dia* was a heavy mass of stodgy reading matter, that was run, only too evidently, for political reasons and in the interests of Spain. It is little wonder, then, that as nine o'clock approached a little flutter of excitement and anticipation manifested itself in the crowds that thronged the cafés and boulevards.

Edward called to a little bare-footed, black-eyed urchin, who was calling his papers, and bought a copy. He had no desire, in his present state, nor did he think it a correct thing, to be seen at any of the fashionable haunts facing the gaily lighted promenade, and he turned and walked slowly up the street, keeping his eye open for a place where he could take his refreshment and read his paper in peace.

He decided upon a corner café that did not seem to be too well patronized, and made his way to one of the little round marble-topped tables sheltered by the glass wind-screen, by which the proprietor protected his guests from the sharp gusts which at times beat through the narrow streets of this part of the town.

Calling a waiter, Edward ordered a coffee and cognac, and, lighting a cigar, opened his paper. It was a badly printed sheet, still damp from the press, and smelling evilly of inferior printers' ink. As he gazed idly down the columns, Edward could well understand the popularity of the wretched rag. Sensation was evidently the keynote of its policy—that and scare and scandal. To the editor of the *Impartial de Corbo* nothing was sacred. Povey read first a long leader on the career of King Enrico, of whose health the reports had the last few days been again more favourable. The tone of the article plainly showed that the editor resented this temporary recovery of a monarch whom he evidently considered to be of more worth dead than on the throne of San Pietro. It mattered nothing to him that the Royal victim of his pen lay dying within a mile of his printing press. Ruthlessly the ruler of San Pietro was attacked—virulently and viciously. His mode of legislature, his family quarrels, his private morals, all came under the lash of the pen. On the question of morals the writer, scenting something to whet the appetite of his readers, had let himself go with a vengeance.

The useful relative in Paris had kept him well supplied with anecdotes and paragraphs relating to Enrico's frequent visits to the French capital. These, while the king had been in good health, he had not dared to publish; but now, when any moment might be the last, he was drawing on the stores of his pigeon-holes, with the result that the café loungers of Corbo were given something to talk about.

Edward put down the paper in disgust. It seemed to his English way of thinking, a poor thing, this attacking of a dying man, who, if report spoke true, must be having a bad enough passing as it was.

He looked up to where, between the gables of the opposite houses, the palace rose up gaunt and sombre above the town. The portion of the building which came within his vision was in darkness, save where in the eastern wing a short row of windows showed little patches of yellow light. It was in those rooms that he understood the dying king lay.

Edward pictured the scene behind those windows, the evil-living man helplessly waiting for what he must hope would be annihilation. He imagined the men round the bed, men intent on plunder, and who could barely wait until the breath left their royal master's body. He wondered what visions were disturbing the king's last hours, and he thought of the many things he had heard of the monarch's past life.

He remembered the tales of murdered and mutilated natives in the rubber plantations of the tiny colony in West Africa which was under the rule of San Pietro. He thought of Enrico's sisters and brothers, all of whom had put their relative out of their lives—and of the heir, travelling where no one knew. The death couch of the King of San Pietro must be an uneasy one indeed.

The words of Fagin ran through his mind as he watched the windows; how did they go—"*as it came on dark, he began to think of all the men he had known who had died.... They rose up in quick succession, that he could hardly count them.*" —Yes, Enrico's last hours must be very like those spent by the old Jew in his Newgate cell.

Edward shuddered a little and took a sip of cognac. Then he picked up the paper again idly and turned to the home news. There were the usual amusement notes and the statistics of play at the tables in the Casino. He read with little interest how a wealthy Austrian nobleman had had a successive run of seventeen on the black, and how he had been forced to have the assistance of one of the attendants to carry the spoil to the hotel.

He looked in vain for an account of the accident on the Alcador road. Galva's death had been soon forgotten, the readers of *El Imparcial de Corbo* were no more interested in it than in the suicide two days previously of the young American, a ruined gambler, who had thrown himself into the sea from the rocks east of the bay.

As he rose to pay his bill, voices at a near table arrested him, and he sat down again and lit the stump of his cigar. Two men, of the middle class, were discussing the motor-car fatality. One of them had remarked how Lieutenant Mozara should have known that road better than to have had such an accident. The speaker himself had seen him often start out that way, and he had a sister, the wife of an innkeeper at Alcador, who had told him that the lieutenant seldom missed the bull-fights that took place periodically in the Plaza of that town. Edward, with his eyes glued to the paper he held before him, drank in every word. It seemed to him corroboration of Anna Paluda's doubts. There was only one direct road to Alcador, and it was difficult to imagine for one moment that such an experienced driver as Lieutenant Mozara undoubtedly was would forget the dangerous bend that wound above the Ardentella rapids.

And yet he said to himself that Gaspar Mozara was scarcely the man to take the risk of the fall. He would be running the same danger as Miranda, and yet here he was in Corbo, to the best of Edward's belief, unhurt. The next words from the adjoining table made matters a little clearer. It was the other man who was speaking now.

"— —I was on the road when they were getting the wrecked car out of the water. I gave them a hand, and, although the machine was badly smashed, one thing struck me as very curious. The brakes had not been applied—whatever happened, the car had gone through the wall at full speed."

The lieutenant's words of the afternoon returned to the man who was listening behind the newspaper, how he had put on the brakes when he had seen the danger. Edward was now convinced that Mozara was lying, but even then he was no nearer the solution of the mystery. Perhaps, after all, Miranda had been in the car, but Edward would not allow himself to think that.

He felt sure that some sign further than the hat and cloak would have been found. It was barely possible that the girl's body would be so separated from the car as to leave a hat and cloak only. It was all but a certainty that she would have been pinned beneath the wreckage. The dainty motor bonnet, too, tied tightly, as he remembered, beneath the chin—how could that have become detached?

No, the more Edward Povey thought of the affair the more certain he became that the girl was being held prisoner by some one who suspected her identity. The lieutenant was, no doubt, acting under the orders of others, and she would be kept in captivity until Dasso, after the king's death, was secure on the throne. Her's was too valuable a life to dispose of, unless it were absolutely necessary.

All these things passed through Edward's mind as he made his way in the direction of Venta Villa. The boulevard was crowded with its usual throng of pleasure seekers. From the interior of the café came the clattering of dishes and the laughter of those who were drinking or supping. Each place, too, had its little orchestra, the uniforms showing hazily through the smoke-laden atmosphere.

As Povey passed the Café de l'Europe, the largest and most fashionable in Corbo, he ran his eyes over the people seated at the little tables. Gaily dressed women smoked cigarettes and drank tiny liqueurs as they joked with bored-looking men in evening attire. Here and there the gorgeous uniform of the King's Own Hussars splashed a note of barbaric colour over the scene.

With a little catch of the breath, Edward suddenly pulled up short and slipped back into the shadow of a newspaper kiosk. From behind this he peeped cautiously at the figure of an elderly gentleman who was seated alone before a table on which stood a stone tankard of Pilsener. Then he passed hastily up the little avenue between the crowded tables and entered the main body of the Café de l'Europe.

Here were blotters containing paper and envelopes, and he drew a sheet towards him and wrote a short note. Then, calling a waiter, he asked him to hand it to the gentleman in the tweed suit who was drinking beer outside. He also, ascertaining that this particular waiter spoke a little English, told the man to tell the gentleman in the tweed suit that the writer of the note would be glad of a word with him in private. Then he leaned back and watched through the large plate-glass windows.

*****

Mr. Jasper Jarman, as the waiter touched him on the shoulder and handed him the note, started violently. For him a touch on the shoulder meant but the one thing, in fact he had been dreaming night and day, ever since his arrival on the island, of touches upon the shoulder.

"Ze gentleman, sir, he speak with m'sieu."

"The devil he will." Jasper Jarman rose hastily and grabbed up his hat and umbrella. "I don't know a soul in the dam island, waiter, and I don't want to. You have made a mistake, my good man."

Jasper unfolded the note as he spoke, and his eye travelled to the signature. He gave a gasp and turned again to the waiter.

"Where is he?"

The man bowed, and pointed to the interior of the café.

"I will show m'sieu."

Edward, however, had risen, and he met his uncle as he edged his way between the crowded tables.

"Not a word here," he said, and, taking the old man's arm, he led him out of the sight of the people, some of whom he noticed were already giving them their attention.

They crossed the crowded pavement and the road to the other side of the promenade. This part, bordered as it was by a low sea wall, and without shops or cafés, was practically deserted, and the two men made their way eastward until they came to a flight of a few shallow steps leading down to the well-kept gardens that were the pride of Corbo.

Edward, still with his hand affectionately linked in his uncle's arm, led the way through shrub-bordered paths to a stone seat that, half hidden in a mass of palm foliage, faced the sea. Here it was quiet, the sound of the promenaders reaching them only in a confused murmur. Little lights gleamed here and there from the yachts anchored in the bay.

"So, uncle, there you are," began Edward, unconsciously quoting Hamlet.

"Yes, Edward Povey, I'm here, through your rotten criminal acts, you—you—jail-bird, you——"

"There is no need, I assure you, my dear Uncle Jasper, to be offensive," said Edward Povey.

CHAPTER XVII.

MR. JASPER JARMAN RELIEVES HIS MIND

There was silence for a few moments. Edward Povey nervously poked little holes in the gravel path with the ferrule of his walking-stick.

"Don't you think, uncle, that we had better discuss the situation without personalities—or rudeness?"

Mr. Jasper Jarman's answer was a grunt.

"You see, uncle, I feel that I owe you some sort of apology, or at any rate an explanation. I read what they said in the papers about you. I laughed for ten minutes."

"You did, eh! Well, I read the same as you did, and I didn't laugh for ten seconds."

"But I didn't take it seriously. I thought you would explain easily."

"Yes, and be convicted as an accessory—as one of the gang."

"Accessory to what?"

"To the theft of the bonds—you did well out of that, it seems." Jasper's eyes took in his nephew's attire, the well-cut dark suit, the gleaming jewel in the cravat. "I suppose you decided on San Pietro for the same reason as I did."

"My dear uncle, I was never more astonished in my life than when I saw you sitting there, outside the Café de l'Europe."

"Not more than I was to see you, Mr. Povey."

Edward sat for a moment gazing out over the sea.

"What I'm wondering at is that a clever business man like you should run away from a shadow."

"Yes, the shadow of a jail—what."

"Not at all, uncle. I read in the Paris *Daily Mail* weeks ago that the bonds had been recovered and that the matter was ended. Why don›t you go back, now?»

"The fact that the bonds are safe does not explain my presence at Adderbury Cottage. I'd have to say I was visiting you—and admit you as my nephew."

"And you wouldn't like that?"

"It's not a relationship that I'm proud of, Edward."

Edward looked at his uncle. "As I remarked before, there's no need to be rude," he said.

"I'm only stating facts, Edward. Remember, I go by what I have seen. What were *you* doing at Bushey, and, for the matter of that, what are you doing here in San Pietro?»

Edward Povey rose and took a turn or two up and down the path. He had asked himself at first whether he had been wise to attract his uncle's attention. But he well knew that until he had found out the reason of the old man's presence on the island, he would know no peace. He was more than relieved to discover the true state of things and that his uncle knew nothing of the Baxendale affair. The best thing to do now was to get the old man back to Kidderminster as soon as possible. There was nothing to associate Edward in his uncle's mind with the Mr. Sydney who lived at Venta Villa, even if, as was hardly probable, that gentleman's name were known to the carpet manufacturer. He pulled up suddenly in his walk as a scheme suggested itself, and stood looking down on Mr. Jarman.

"I really think, uncle, you had better go back and face the music— it's a bit late, I'll admit, but it's your best move."

"And face the scandal too. Not me."

"There won't be any scandal if you do as I say. Write a letter to the editor of your local paper—*The Kidderminster Shuttle*, isn't it? Tell him that you have been on a long sea voyage by your doctor's orders and that you haven't been able to write or receive letters for weeks. Say that you have just read in an old number of the *Daily Telegraph* that you have been ‹wanted.› Work up the indignation hot and strong— say that you are hastening home to take proceedings for libel against any one who has said a word against you. You must, also, say that Kyser was a friend of yours and that he had lent you the cottage at Bushey, and that when Aunt Eliza heard he was murdered, she was frightened of ghosts and that is why you left so hurriedly. Say she wouldn't sleep another night in the place for a fortune."

Edward paused and wiped the perspiration from his face. Jasper, who had been looking glum enough when his nephew had begun to speak, now raised his head with a little smile.

"You're a magnificent liar, Edward—same time I rather like your idea—I believe you possess the elements of sense."

Edward smiled his acknowledgments, then went on—

"But I have a favour to ask, uncle. Forget you've seen me. I'm here on business—secret political business."

"I shan't say a word. Get me out of this benighted place and I'll do anything you like. Now come on with me to my hotel and I'll write that letter."

The two men left the gardens and walked up towards the Old Town.

"I'm staying at The Three Lilies, a comfortable old place—nothing grand and smart like these"—Jasper waved to the great hotels on the front,—"but I wanted somewhere quiet, you see."

"The Three Lilies? Is that the little inn that faces an old castle sort of a place—just on the edge of the Old Town?"

"Yes—why?"

"Oh, nothing. I'm only wondering if you have noticed anything strange about that old place opposite."

"Well—they seem rather a queer lot. Men—mostly soldiers— come pretty often to see the man who lives there. They come secretly too; there was one the other night who hid in the yard under my window. I heard something and looked out; you can understand the fright I got when I saw the tip of a man's cigar."

"What kind of a man was he? Can you describe him?"

"I watched after I had put the light out. There was a horse standing at the door opposite and the owner of the place came and saw a man— another soldier—off the premises. When the sound of the horse had died away in the distance, the man under my window crossed over. I've often seen him."

"Sallow face, eh? Thin?"

"That fits him. He's been in the wars, however. I saw him to-day and he walks with a crutch and carries his arm in a sling. Why? Do you know the Johnny who lives in the castle?"

Edward did not answer; he was thinking deeply. These clandestine meetings between Mozara and Dasso were only in accordance with the suspicions that crowded his mind of a plot. A great joy filled his heart as he told himself that Miranda was alive. He was glad he had written to the Duc de Choleaux Lasuer, a strong arm to lean on would be useful in the work Edward Povey had in hand.

It was late when they reached The Three Lilies and the house opposite was in darkness. Edward accompanied his uncle to his room and together they wrote their letter to *The Kidderminster Shuttle*. This done, the younger man took his departure. He made an appointment with his uncle at the stone seat in the gardens for eleven o'clock the next morning. He was rather sorry he had advised the old man to hurry away; he would have been useful as an informant, living as he did with the enemy under his eye.

Any schemes such as these, however, were doomed to have a very rude awakening. Edward arrived at the stone seat early and gave himself up to his thoughts. His original misdemeanour in assuming the name and personality of Mr. Kyser was all but forgotten in the light of later events, and the plans for the location and rescue of Galva Baxendale. In his own mind he was rather more than half a hero already, and the shock which he received at five minutes past eleven was a sharp one, and coming, as it did, hard upon his self-adulation seemed to him unmerited and unfair.

As steps approached he looked up expecting to see the portly figure of Mr. Jasper Jarman. Instead, he made out a lean and hungry looking Corbian who, when he saw the figure on the seat, advanced, and snatching off his greasy cap handed a letter to Edward.

"Meester Povee?"

Edward took the envelope and opening it drew out a sheet of paper. It was dated at nine o'clock in the morning and was headed with the device THE THREE LILIES.

"EDWARD POVEY,

"Please accept my very best thanks for the advice you gave me yesterday evening. You have in some measure atoned for the harm you have done. On your head and yours alone rests the onus of my shattered reputation, the anguish of your Aunt Eliza and the possible downfall of one of the largest carpet factories in the Midlands.

"Last night circumstances made it expedient that I should dissemble and show you a tolerance I was far from feeling. You are a liar and I do not doubt for one moment but that you are a thief. It was to avoid the possible trial with such a scoundrel beside me in the dock that I left England. When you get this I shall have departed from the cursed island of San Pietro by the boat that leaves for Spain at ten. You did not mention your poor wife to me. I do not expect I will run across her, it being more than probable that you have murdered the poor woman and buried her in the garden at Adderbury Cottage. If I do see her, however, I will consider it my duty to acquaint her with the evil life of self-indulgence and ease you are living in Corbo.

"The messenger who brings you this is the son of the landlord of The Three Lilies. I have told him that you will reward him — you can afford it.

"JASPER JARMAN"

Edward tore the letter into little pieces and swore softly to himself. It was a rude awakening to his dreams of rescuing distressed damsels. Then he took a silver coin from his pocket and handed it to the son of the landlord of The Three Lilies.

"There's no answer," he said shortly, and turned and walked up to the bustling life of the boulevard. He had entered the gardens with the feelings of Sir Galahad, he left them with those of Charles Peace.

CHAPTER XVIII.

THE CAPTIVE

In the early part of the seventeenth century a certain noble duchess, taking a journey through the kingdom of San Pietro, paid a visit to her old and valued friend the Countess Ribero, and the guest-chamber in which the august lady spent two nights has since been called the Duchess Room, and it was upon the faded glories of this distinguished apartment that the bewildered eyes of poor Galva Baxendale looked when she came out of her insensibility.

The moon shining obliquely in at the long windows flooded parts of the room in a white light, mercilessly picking out the threadbare patches in the ragged tapestries and in the faded embroideries of the chair-backs. A fire burning brightly in the grate somewhat relieved the cold splendour of the moonbeams.

Galva was, for a few moments, oblivious to her surroundings. Her head throbbed and ached distractingly, and she gazed with unseeing eyes at the carved oaken pillars of the four-post bed on which she was lying, and on the heavy curtains and fringes which hemmed her in. Her first distinct impression was one of suffocation. She had that horror, so common to those who have lived in and love the open air, of all enclosed spaces and smothering draperies.

She raised herself slowly, and leaning her head on her hand, took a survey of the surrounding objects. The room was a large one, and was lighted by two windows, reaching nearly to the ground, and composed of many small square panes. On the walls the tarnished frames of pictures, mostly portraits, caught the firelight. Facing her was a large tapestry on which were depicted the figures of three huntsmen, with very thin legs, who, accompanied by prancing dogs, were presumably chasing a stag, which was conveniently silhouetted on the top of a symmetrical mountain.

As Galva put her foot to the ground the ludicrous figures seemed to take life and accompany the furniture and the bed in a whirling, fantastic dance, and the girl felt her senses again leaving her. But she must have tottered somehow to the window, for the next she remembered was the cool night breezes of the forest, pine-scented and invigorating, playing upon her forehead. With each inhalation Galva felt her strength coming back to her, and the memory of all that had happened returned to her in every detail.

She remembered Mozara and the car, and how, much against her will, he had insisted on running her out to see the Falls on the Ardentella. She had known that it was a very different thing the journey inland, without a chaperone, to the quiet gliding up and down the promenade at Corbo. She knew also that her guardian did not altogether approve of even this latter, and as the powerful car had bounded on past the palace, she had implored the lieutenant to take her back.

But the young man would not believe she was serious and had laughed at her fears. They would be back in an hour, he had told her, and so, helpless, she had made the best of it, promising herself a sharp retaliation on her escort when she was safely home again.

Galva remembered stopping at a lonely spot where two gate-posts stood sentinel by the side of the road. There was a wood, too, comprised, as far as she could recollect, of pine-trees. Mozara had here alighted to attend to his engine, and after propping open the bonnet had gone back to the tonneau, saying he wanted to get a spanner from the tool-bag he kept there. There was a confused memory after that of a cloth being swathed about her head and the sickly sweet smell of chloroform. Then nothing more—until she had come to herself in this old-world room.

She raised her head in the act of listening and tiptoed to the door. She could detect stealthy movements on the landing outside, and through a little crack in the oaken panel came the gleam of a light.

Galva was no coward. She had the heart of the Estratos and a line of ancestors whose deeds of bravery were chronicled back to the dim ages. But there was something uncanny in this weird room, with the flickering firelight the cold moon and the unknown silent watchers on the landing. Then she heard the footsteps creep away, and, unable to bear the suspense longer, the girl seized the handle of the door and shook it furiously. She tried to call out, to ask who was there, but her tongue seemed a useless lump in her dry mouth, and sound would not come.

The footsteps outside stopped at the first sound of the rattled door, and Galva heard whispered voices. Then a key grated in the lock, and the girl retreated to the farther end of the room. At the first sound she had taken from her pocket a tiny revolver, hardly more than a toy, which Edward, not knowing what was in store for them in San Pietro, had bought for her in Paris. She saw the door slowly opened and an old man enter. Behind him Teresa carried a tray on which were a flask of wine and some covered dishes.

"You are ready for supper, señorita?"

Galva gazed wonderingly at them. All fear had left her now, and she fingered her revolver confidently. The firelight glinted on the little plated barrel and threw gigantic shadows of the old couple on the yellow ceiling. She was speaking in a low voice which she would hardly have recognized as her own.

"Put the tray down," every word came distinctly, "and then stand over there—where I can see you both. Then tell me what this all means."

Pieto looked at his wife hesitatingly, and pointed to the tray. Teresa set it down.

"Now," went on the girl, "I want a full explanation—where is Lieutenant Mozara? I don't think I know either of you—do I?"

"The lieutenant has left the castle."

"It seems that the lieutenant has played a trick on me—a trick that will cost him dear—and," meaningly, "those who are with him in it."

The old people stood with bowed heads and the man mumbled something below his breath.

"Speak up, man."

Pieto raised palsied finger-tips to his mouth. "We are not the servants of Lieutenant Mozara," he said.

Galva stamped her little shoe.

"Then go to the man who is your master, whoever he is, and tell him to come to me here. If either of you two enter this room again without my full permission I will shoot you down like I would a couple of dangerous dogs—now go."

Taking up the lantern which he had set down on the floor on entering the room, the old man made for the door, forcing himself in front of his wife in his anxiety to get clear of the little vixen who could hold a revolver so straight and steady. Teresa gave Galva a long and searching look, then she too followed her craven lord and master.

And Galva gave a little laugh as she found herself alone again. She took the cover from one of the dishes and bent her head over the contents. Whatever could be said of the old dame downstairs Galva noticed with satisfaction that she was no amateur in the art of the kitchen, and the dainty meal was soon eaten with the relish of a healthy fourteen-hour hunger. For the captive told herself that everything depended upon her having the strength to seize any advantage in her position that might occur.

She went again to the open window and looking out judged that she was some twenty-five feet above the ground level, but that below that again ran a moat-like trench, dug perhaps to allow light to the cellars. She thought of the curtains, estimating their length with her eye; they might perhaps reach the twenty-five feet, but there was no way of crossing the trench. True, the portico of the building was only perhaps fifteen feet below her, but it lay some distance to the left and was quite inaccessible.

Galva glanced at the little strap watch on her wrist and saw that it was past ten. From below stairs there came no sound, and she told herself that her jailers had retired for the night, and, again with the view of husbanding her strength, the prisoner prepared to follow their example.

While at supper she had heard the stealthy footsteps again outside her door and the grating of bolts hastily shot into their sockets. It was evident that escape was not to be thought of that night.

The glass of excellent Chianti that she had taken with her meal had quite restored her courage and spirits, and she began to look upon the adventure as rather interesting. It seemed clear to her that whoever was responsible for the outrage meant her no immediate harm, and she had no fear whatever of the old couple down below.

With some little difficulty she piled three of the heavy oak chairs by the door as a precaution against a midnight surprise, and taking off only her outer garments and her shoes, slipped in between the sheets. The fire, which she had replenished from the heap of logs in the grate, shone dully on the rich old furnishings of the room and gave a sense of drowsy comfort and well-being. Candles and matches she found on a little table which she pushed up near the bed. The revolver lay handy underneath her pillow. Miss Galva, in fact, was very comfortable indeed, and had it not been for the thought of her guardian and Anna Paluda and the anxiety they must be feeling, she would have been really happy.

It was broad day when she awoke and the birds in the forest were making merry music. The sun shone in at the windows and gave life to the somewhat sombre apartment. Galva's watch told her it was nine o'clock.

She was feeling remarkably well, her headache had entirely left her, and she was ravenously hungry again. A sound outside the window caused her to slip on her garments and look out. Beneath her the little patch of poor soil that lay between the house and the trees had been, at parts, coaxed into a cultivation of sorts, and the old woman who the night before had brought her supper was gathering some kind of green stuff, putting it into the basket that she carried slung over her arm. From her window, too, the girl could see over the trees to the country beyond—an arid rock-strewn waste and here and there patches of forest land. Away in the distance the range of the Yeldo hills showed a delicate mauve against the morning sky.

Galva watched the old woman for a moment in silence, then—

"Good-morning, Teresa." The girl had heard the name the evening before, and on the old woman looking up, she nodded brightly. "Is breakfast ready, Teresa?" she went on.

The old woman dipped her head sourly.

"Pieto shall bring it up to you," she said.

"Thanks, so much—but, by the way, tell him to take great care how he does it. Listen. He is to bring it in on a tray which he will set down on the little table here. Then he will hold up his hands, both of them, over his head and walk out backwards."

Teresa was making her way slowly towards the house, giving scant attention to the voice above her. Galva raised her voice.

"You understand, don't you, Teresa? Because if your husband doesn't do as he's told, I'll have to shoot him."

The woman in the garden stopped at this and looked up.

"You would shoot my Pieto?"

"Oh, don't be afraid, Teresa; I'd only shoot him in the leg. Then you'd have to nurse him, you know, and that would be a pity, wouldn't it? Think of keeping an eye on a prisoner and an invalid at the same time."

Galva never forgot the pantomime of the next few minutes. Covered by the revolver, the old man shuffled unsteadily into the room with the tray, splashing the white cloth with the contents of the coffee pot. Then, after putting it down where Galva bid him, he began his retreat, backwards, hands held high over his head. Near the door he came to grief with a crash over one of the chairs his prisoner had used as a barricade the night before. The old man remembered to keep his hands up, and the species of contortions, reminiscent of Swedish exercises, with, which he tried to regain his feet brought tears of laughter into Galva's eyes. He was successful at last, and the girl heard his limping steps descend the stairs, where, with many curses, he seemed to be, as Galva expressed it to herself, "taking it out of the missus!"

Left alone the prisoner poured herself out a cup of fragrant coffee.

"There seems to be a humorous side to even this adventure," she said as she contentedly nibbled at a piece of buttered toast.

CHAPTER XIX.

TERESA

As day succeeded monotonous day, even Galva's buoyant spirits began to show signs of the strain of hope deferred. The first hours of her captivity had given her little or no uneasiness, feeling sure that her friends would discover her whereabouts; if they did not, she told herself that, armed as she was, she was more than a match for the two craven souls of her jailers.

But on the second night she had heard the sound of a new voice in the room down-stairs, whether one voice or more she could not say. Also the sound of a motor-horn had come to her through the woods. This latter she had not given much thought to at the time, thinking that in all probability it was a car on its way to Alcador. Now that there were visitors in the room below, the memory came back to her and took on a new significance.

Whoever it was who was responsible for this muttering that reached her distantly through the floor, he did not seem anxious for an interview with her. She had pounded on the boards with the heel of her shoe, but beyond a short silence and a little laugh it had had no effect, and the murmuring voices went on again as before. Then she had turned her attention to the heavy fire-irons, and the continued din had brought old Pieto to the landing to remonstrate through the door, and to assure the girl, in answer to her questions, that there was no one in the house save themselves.

But a little later, Galva had heard the opening of the front door and, in the distance, the sound of a motor-engine being started.

The next morning, she had seen a man digging in the little vegetable patch, a coarse, black-browed, evil-faced fellow. Galva remembered having seen the same type of man, with their closely-cropped heads, among the loafers outside the bull-rings in Madrid, and she knew their reputation. She drew back into the room, and for the first time since her capture, her heart failed her. Where were her friends, and why did they not come to her?

Her mind flew, in its need, to the Duc de Choleaux Lasuer, and she told herself, and thrilled at the telling, that he would rush to her assistance did he know. He had asked her on that last day in Paris to write to him, should she be in any trouble, and she, seeing no clouds in her future, had laughed at him. Now she shut her eyes and saw again the eager boyish face, and she knew what a big place he had in her heart.

She threw herself down on the great bed and buried her face in the pillow. The tears that came were the first she had shed and they relieved her. The knowledge that all escape by force was impossible took from her the thoughts that had buoyed her up. Now, she could not tell how many there were against her, and she knew that the man she had seen in the garden was not one to be cowed by a girl with a toy pistol.

She sat up and dried her eyes. What could not be done one way, must be done another. She must think out some scheme, some subterfuge to gain her release. If only she could get a letter or a message sent to Venta Villa. The high road ran only a hundred yards from her window, but the hundred yards might be miles for all the use they were, so securely was her retreat hidden. Of the imaginary accident and of her supposed death she of course knew nothing.

After this the days passed with a dull monotony. The prisoner, seeing that no good was to be expected of it, dropped her bantering tone with the old people. No longer were her meals served to her at the pistol point. For hours together she would sit, a pathetic little figure, in the great arm-chair which she had pulled into the embrasure of one of the windows, not even turning her head when Pieto or his wife entered. She would sit there gazing out across the tree-tops to the arid plains and the wild desolation of the distant hills. There were dark circles showing now under the beautiful eyes, and sometimes the meals were taken away again untasted.

And then a little gleam of hope came to her. Since her first arrival at the little castle she had noticed the covert looks, half admiration, half fear, with which Teresa had regarded her. Twice, too, she had seen that the old woman had been on the point of saying something that was in her mind, but each time she had checked herself and broken off with a sigh. One day Galva spoke to her.

It was a dull and miserable morning, with a fine rain that lashed and blurred the windowpanes, and a high wind moaned through the trees of the forest, swaying their topmost branches. Teresa was leaving the room with the scarcely touched breakfast when Galva laid a gentle hand on her arm.

"Teresa," she whispered.

The dame stopped and looked at her. Galva thought she saw compassion in the beady black eyes.

"Teresa—you are a woman and have a heart. I have seen your heart sometimes in your eyes, when you look at me. Have you no pity there for me? All this is killing me—I am ill, Teresa—I have lived my life in the open air of God's green world, and this," with a despairing gesture that took in all the room, "is weighing on me—killing—crushing me."

Teresa swallowed something in her throat.

"I had a heart, but I thought it dead—and you say you can see it in my eyes. How can I help you? I act for others."

"I am rich, Teresa, you can have anything you wish for. Let me write a letter to my friends. Think of their anxiety. Here," and the girl tore at the bosom of her blouse, snapping a thin ribbon that passed round her neck, "take this now—it's valuable, Teresa, very valuable. See, they are diamonds, and that big red stone is a ru——"

Galva broke off and gazed in wonderment at the old woman. At sight of the glittering object which the girl with trembling hands held out, a sudden change had come into the wrinkled face. She seized on the large marquise ring and looked at it intently, searchingly, but there was no cupidity in her glance, only a great dawning wonderment. She turned roughly on the bewildered girl, bringing her old eyes within a foot of her face.

"Who are you?" she asked, her voice a hoarse whisper. "For God's sake—tell me—who are you?"

"I am Miss Galva Baxendale, that is, I—I—— Oh, I see that you know. I can tell by your face that you do."

"I do now. I know that you are the Princess Miranda. I suspected before, and my suspicion has grown every time I saw your eyes. But I told myself that I was getting old and that I saw things that did not exist—only in my brain."

Teresa was on her knees, pressing Galva's hand to her cold lips.

"It was this ring—the sainted Queen who wore it. Oh, how can I tell you——"

The old woman was crying softly now, and she had not cried for nearly twenty years. In a little while she grew more composed and went to the landing and listened.

"They are at their cards," she said, when she returned, "and Pieto is drunk; they will not disturb us," and then Teresa told her story.

"You said to-night that you saw the heart that died—for my heart died seventeen years ago when I buried my José. He was only five, but he never walked. He would just lie in the sun in his little wheeled cradle and look up at the sky and smile at me with his deep eyes and ask me things I could not tell him. Pieto, too, in those days was a good father and loved his little crippled son almost as much as I did. And then one day there was a jingling of harness and Queen Elene drove past our little house, that lay up on the cliff road towards Logillo. She ordered her postilions to stop and called me to the side of the carriage. She had the sweetest smile that ever told of a perfect soul, and tender eyes into which came a mist when I answered her questions about little José.

"And then she got down and knelt in the dust beside the cradle, and the little man looked at her with his great wondering eyes, and put up his thin little hand to touch the glittering ornaments at the Queen's neck. And after that she often drove that way, and would sit with him. Once she told me of her own little child, a maid—but I think she thought it unkind to speak of her own blessings in the face of my sorrow, for she only spoke of you that once."

Teresa held out her hand and took up the ring that she had laid down on the tray.

"This was what he admired more than anything, and your mother would take it from her finger and let him play with it, flashing it back and forth in the sunlight. The day before he died she had lent it to him and he had gone to sleep still holding it. The Queen would not awake him, and in the night he died. When, afterwards, I returned it to the Queen, she wept; she would have had me keep it, but it was, she said, the first gift your father had given her. That is my story—and you, Princess? I do not want to know how you escaped the fate of that devilish work at the Palace. I know only, that you are here and that I ask nothing better than to die for you, for the sake of your sainted mother, and for the joy she brought into my boy's life."

Galva, her eyes moist with tears, bent and kissed the wrinkled brow.

"And I, Teresa, want you to live. I think I want you always to be with me, to talk to me about my mother."

Teresa shook her head. "I am not worthy," she said. "After José was taken from us, Pieto took to the drink, and I—I did not care what happened. We took service with Gabriel Dasso—it was rumoured that his was the hand that killed the Queen. We hoped to gain evidence that it was so, and we would have poisoned him. But we learnt nothing. We obeyed him and did his dirty work, sinking lower and lower until we forgot why we had entered his service. I am not worthy, Princess, to touch the sole of your shoe."

Galva rose.

"I won't write the letter till this afternoon, Teresa. You can get it through to Corbo for me?"

"There is a carrier, Princess, who passes here twice a week, about nightfall. He reaches Corbo at eleven. To-morrow is his next journey. I will see that he takes your letter."

"And you will come and sit with me, Teresa—we have much to talk over, haven't we? It will do you good, dear. Do not let them see down-stairs that you have been crying. For the present you must keep our secret."

When Teresa had left the room, Galva crossed over, and leaning her elbows on the mantelpiece looked long and searchingly at herself in the mirror.

CHAPTER XX.

THE BOAT FROM THE MAINLAND

If the days hung heavily upon the heart of the captive in the castle on the Alcador road, they hung no less heavily upon the man who waited in Venta Villa.

The culpability of one's actions is too often determined by the worldly success, or otherwise, which attends them, and Edward Povey was experiencing some very bitter moments. Had Galva been firmly and happily seated in the great throne-room up there in the Palace, he would have carried his head high and have looked upon himself as a hero, and his usurpation of the character of Sydney Kyser as a meritorious act.

But under the existing circumstances he cursed himself for a meddlesome idiot, or worse, and prayed that he might suddenly awake to find himself dozing over the corner desk in the dingy Eastcheap counting-house or in his shabby arm-chair in the front room at Belitha Villas.

Hitherto he had accepted his present luxurious surroundings as due to him for the trouble he was taking; now each item of them became a stab. The well-cooked dinners which he took miserably with Anna Paluda seemed like to choke him, and the dainty hangings of his little bedroom, overlooking the bay, became a physical torture to him. The letter sent him by Jasper Jarman also rankled deeply. He wished he had kept the letter now, that he might read it again and again as a penance.

By a stroke of ill-fortune Señor Luazo was confined to his room with an attack of gout, and the fashionable physician who attended that estimable gentleman had made it clear to Edward that his patient was not to be disturbed. Any help or even advice from that quarter was out of the question.

But Mr. Povey had not been content to rest in idleness; as far as it was possible he had acted. Disguised, he had ingratiated himself with the landlord of The Three Lilies, and had spent hours together behind the little curtain of the window of the room vacated by Uncle Jasper, which overlooked the house and gardens of Gabriel Dasso. He had, however, gained little by this, save one important point, the certainty that Lieutenant Mozara was, without doubt, malingering in the matter of his injuries.

The gallant officer, thinking himself secure behind the high walls of Dasso's garden, had relaxed his precautions. Twice the watchful eye at the window opposite had seen the crutch discarded and the black silk sling hanging empty.

Beyond the comfort derived from this confirmation of the suspicions which Anna Paluda had planted in his mind, Edward could make no use of the information gained. Any day now he might receive an answer to the letter he had sent to M. Brea in Paris, and until that came he was loath to act. He felt that, with the help of the Duc de Choleaux Lasuer, he would be more than a match for the conspirators. At the same time, for Galva's sake, he determined that should no word reach him within the next three days he would put the matter before the British Consul.

He had met the monocled nonentity who represented the interests of Great Britain in the island kingdom. Señor Luazo had introduced them in the café attached to the Casino, and Edward had not been impressed. The Consul did not appear to him to be the man to lean on in any great emergency. Commerce between the idle inhabitants of San Pietro and English ports was confined to the few boxes of dried fruits of two Jewish firms in the business quarter of Corbo, and the Government post in the service of His Britannic Majesty on the little island was not one sought after by ambitious men. No, on second thoughts, Edward did not feel inclined to disturb the alcohol-engendered ease of the Honourable Bertie Traverson unless it became absolutely necessary.

The evening following the day on which Teresa learnt the identity of Galva Baxendale, Edward was sitting in the little library at Venta

Villa, reading for the hundredth time a telegram which he had that morning received. A knock at the door caused him to crumple this up guiltily in his hands as the servant entered. A man was at the door asking for Mr. Sydney—rather a curious person, the servant volunteered, respectfully. Edward, eager for anything to relieve the period of waiting, went out into the hall. A rough individual was there, standing on the mat, his clothes dripping and making little rain-pools on the tiled floor.

As he saw Edward he bowed a black shaggy head, and from the sodden recesses of his heavy coat produced a dirty envelope which he held out. Edward could see it was addressed to Mr. Sydney, at the Venta Villa, Corbo. The light in the hall was not good, and Povey stepped back into the library to open and read the letter. A moment later he was again out in the hall, calling to the servant to bring wine for the messenger. To his surprise the man had disappeared, the little pools of water alone remaining to show where he had stood. Edward flung open the door. The wind swept the rain in his face in clouds, and that, together with the darkness, made the man's retreat secure. Having rid himself of the letter entrusted to him, the carrier of the Alcador road considered he had done all that could be expected of him. Remembering the air of mystery with which Teresa had given him the envelope, he wished to be done with the affair. Curiosity was not one of his failings, and the suspiciously generous payment the old woman had made him was burning in his pockets with a flame that called for the extinguishing wine of a little inn he knew, nestling beneath the shadow of the cathedral.

Edward Povey cleared the flight of richly carpeted stairs in three bounds and burst frantically into the little drawing-room. The black-gowned figure in the arm-chair, drawn up to the fire, rose at his entrance and stood facing him inquiringly; one arm resting on the chair-back, with the other she pressed a lace handkerchief to her lips. The room was lighted by a single cluster of electric bulbs only, but Edward could see that Anna Paluda's face was chalky-grey, and that the large eyes looked tired with tears.

"She's found, Anna. Galva's safe."

The woman thanked God and reached out a trembling hand for the letter. Edward switched on the other lights, and together they devoured Galva's message. As they finished reading it the second time the chimes of the cathedral clock reached them.

"Twelve o'clock, Anna. Nothing can be done to-night. And the rain—listen to it."

Anna sat silent for a moment gazing out through the blurred panes at the inky blackness beyond. The rain lashed the windows like a shower of sand, and the waves breaking on the shore below voiced a distant monotony. Edward was right, nothing could be done at once, except to go to bed and get what rest one might against the morrow.

Left alone, Povey took out the telegram he had been reading and had hastily thrust into his jacket pocket on the entrance of the servant. He smoothed it out on a little table. It was from the Duc de Choleaux Lasuer, and as Edward read it again he told himself that he was nearing the end of his tribulations.

He had been rather averse to showing the cable to Anna. She knew nothing of the affection, if it can be called only that, which existed between Galva and the duke, or if she had noticed it in Paris it had long ago left her memory. Edward doubted whether she would think it wise, this calling in of a stranger to their affairs.

The message was quite brief, and stated simply that the sender had reached Spain and was leaving by the boat which was due to arrive at Port Corbo at nine that evening. Edward had waited anxiously in the rain until the harbour master had told him that the heavy weather had delayed the sturdy little vessel, which acted as passenger, cargo and mail steamer between the island and the mainland. The man had said that she had not yet passed the Point at the arm of the bay where the alternate red and white flashes of the distant lighthouse showed dimly through the driving rain. Edward had learnt that she could not berth before two in the morning, and he had returned to the Villa for refreshment and dry clothes.

At one o'clock he quietly ascertained that Anna had retired for the night, then, putting on a long mackintosh, crept from the house and started on the mile or more walk to the dock side. The rain had now nearly ceased, and the esplanade lay a glistening line of wet asphalt in front of him, in which the arc lamps threw a clean reflection. The wind still blew in fitful gusts, scattering the raindrops from the leaves of the trees that bordered the pavement.

The promenade was deserted, save for a few waiting motor-cars and carriages outside the Casino. From time to time a whistle would call one of these up to the entrance, and Edward would catch a glimpse of black-coated men holding umbrellas over the dainty figures of lightly cloaked women who, with skirts well bunched up over slender ankles and high-heeled shoes, made a dash for the carriage door.

And here and there were shuffling figures edging along in the shadows. These were the denizens of the hinterland of Corbo, night-birds who crept out to the fashionable haunts in the dark hours, bent on plunder, or perhaps the honest earning of a little of the money which was being so freely spent there.

Past the Opera House and the gardens the way became darker. The arc lamps became further apart, and the few cafés that were still open showed sleepy waiters standing moodily behind the great plate-glass windows, waiting for the stragglers to depart.

As Edward walked on he thought of the coming interview, debating within himself whether or no he should acquaint the new arrival with the true state of affairs. He felt that the secret was not altogether his own, and now that he had heard from Galva that she was safe and in no immediate danger, he said that there was no need to act hurriedly. He rather wished, in fact, that he had not been so hasty in writing. The duke would be useful certainly, but he complicated matters.

As he neared the dock the way became increasingly difficult. The Powers that Be in the Island of San Pietro made up for their lavish pandering to their rich visitors by altogether neglecting those portions of the town that lay remote from the Casino. Short, narrow streets, the houses of which seemed tumbling in on one in the darkness, straggled down to the waterside. In places, the particular road which Edward had taken was so steep that rough slabs of granite had been crudely laid down in a series of steps, broad and shallow, down which he stumbled dangerously.

The houses, for the most part, were in darkness, save where here and there an open door silhouetted the shrouded figure of a woman who would whisper to him as he hurried past. A party of Swedish sailors were quarrelling under the hanging oil-lamp of an inn, the doors of which were being hastily shut and bolted. Edward passed unnoticed, and in a moment emerged on the broad cobbled wharf.

Here, doubtless with a view of favourably impressing arriving visitors, the Powers that Be proved more prodigal with illumination, and a row of arc lamps showed the misty forms of a few tramp steamers huddled up to the dock edge. A little knot of seamen and luggage touts stood looking out towards the open sea. From one of the boats a wheezy concertina was accompanying a rich tenor voice singing an old English ballad.

His friend, the harbour master, was not to be seen, but Edward learnt from one of the seamen that the Spanish boat was expected to be alongside in the course of half an hour. He could hear the syren booming dismally.

Edward Povey buried his chin more deeply between the storm-collars of his mackintosh and waited, pacing up and down in the raw, damp mist.

CHAPTER XXI.

EDWARD SEES COMPLICATIONS

Galva had written—

".... so, as I hardly expect you will be able to get a reply through to me, I had better make my own arrangements. At ten o'clock each night I will be in readiness and Teresa will be on hand to open the door to you on your giving the signal, Anna and I, in dear old Cornwall, used, when we became separated in any way, to call to each other by imitating the cry of the kestrel. I will wait for that signal here. You must remember that I have promised old Teresa that her husband will come to no harm ... I am well and in no danger, and having allayed your anxiety and eased my mind, I can wait quite happily till you come...."

The captive had set forth at length the manner of her capture and the position of Casa Luzo. She had briefly touched upon the friendship for her shown by Teresa and how the old woman had discovered her secret. She impressed upon Edward to lay his plans well and not to spoil matters by undue haste.

"Casa Luzo," murmured the Duc de Choleaux Lasuer, "it lies nine or ten miles out on the Alcad..."

"You know the Alcador road, duke?"

The boyish face flushed a little and his grace bent over Galva's letter.

"A little," he said. "An idle man of the world like myself knows most of the pleasure spots on this old earth of ours—I had my car over here last year and I did a lot of work on these inland roads."

They were sitting on the balcony outside the drawing-room windows of Venta Villa. The duke had, immediately upon his arrival in the early hours of the morning, hurried Edward away from the lighted dock-side up to the house, keeping ever on the darker side of the way. Edward had noticed with no little alarm, how, under some pretext or other, he had contrived to keep his features hidden when any one approached. He would stop and light his cigarette, or stoop and occupy himself with his bootlace. Edward, whom recent affairs had made observant, did not feel at all comfortable.

It was plain to him that his grace was anxious that he should not be observed, and he felt uneasy to think that there could be any mystery about the young man on whom he was depending for so much help. He decided that, for the present, the least said was soonest mended, and he would not share the secret of Galva's birth with him until he could more clearly see his way.

But now, as he looked at the figure of the young man beside him on the balcony and noted the frank open countenance, the steady eye, he felt a pang of compunction at doubting him. And yet—why was it that the duke had taken up his position behind the thick fronds of the largest palm that adorned the little balcony? A coincidence perhaps, but— —

The mistral-like storm of the night before had passed over, leaving Corbo radiant and clean in the bright sunlight. The sea was calming and there was no wind. The sun had been strong, and now in the early afternoon there was not a spot of moisture left on the promenade.

"There will be a moon to-night, Mr. Sydney."

"Good—and you really think it better not to risk the road?"

The duke drew a large scale map of Corbo and its surroundings towards him.

"It's unnecessary. The Sebastin Park, so Señora Paluda says, merges into the forest, and once there the way seems clear. The distance appears to be less that way, and I do not think we can go wrong. We will leave ourselves plenty of time."

A meal was taken at three o'clock and immediately afterwards the men set out, each armed with a revolver. They did not consider it needful to take other help with them—secrecy was half the battle. Edward felt his misgivings returning to him in full force as he noticed that, in spite of the warm sun, the duke twisted a thick muffler round his neck, burying his chin and mouth in the folds.

The Sebastin Park, given to the people of San Pietro by their late ill-fated king, was a magnificent stretch of vivid lawns and trim gravel paths. The semi-tropical vegetation was trained and cultivated to show to the best advantage and everywhere little statues and fountains gleamed white in the sun. There were, also, on the outer edges of the park, walks more secluded and screened by shrubberies of rhododendrons.

Edward frowned as he noticed that his companion chose these outer pathways in preference to the broad walks, where nursemaids and their little charges swarmed and idle promenaders walked slowly up and down. With chin buried in his muffler, the Duc de Choleaux Lasuer walked quickly, his eyes nervously looking from side to side.

And then they were in the forest. The cultivation was left behind and there was only a little zigzag path winding between the trunks of the great pines. Through them to the left a glimpse of the grey walls of the Palace grounds showed sombre against the sky. Edward pointed this out to the duke and spoke of the dying king. He detected a shadow pass over the boyish face, and the duke's next remark was on an entirely different subject. A suspicion of the truth was born in Edward's mind at that moment.

But the brisk action and the clean scents of the woodland drove all thoughts save those of Galva from his mind and filled him with the spirit of romance and the joy of living. Uncle Jasper's letter was forgotten and Edward became again, in his own eyes, the knight-errant and hero.

They reached the precincts of the Casa Luzo from the back and long before they had expected. Edward's watch told them that it was eight o'clock, and the men had to wait with what patience they could the passing of the next two hours. They took their places upon a fallen tree trunk in a clearing, and lit cigarettes and looked at the moon rising over the Yeldo hills and at the black and green mystery of the forest around them. The silence was intense and neither of the waiting men seemed anxious to break the magic of it.

And then as it grew chilly they reconnoitred, taking stock of their position. They made a wide detour of the house, penetrating deeply into the wood. They saw not a soul, but once the eerie glow of a charcoal-burner splashed redly between the trees.

At five minutes to the hour they stood just within the belt of trees facing the house. Edward's first attempt at the kestrel's note was not a success. The weird sound echoed dismally through the night, awaking the bird life to protesting cries. He cleared his throat and tried again,—then, as the surrounding birds quieted down into a peevish chatter, a window on the first floor showed a faint light.

As they watched, grotesque shadows flitted over the ceiling and walls within the room as the occupant carried the candle to the window. For a moment Galva's slender form showed silhouetted against the glow,—then darkness. The men crept quietly up to the building.

As they mounted the steps they saw the massive door before them slowly open a few inches. Edward put out his hand and gently pushed it, and they were inside the hall.

It was in darkness, save for the dull glow that came from a horn lantern that stood on the stone floor. By its fitful light they could make out the shadowy form of an old woman who stood regarding them from the foot of the staircase. The rays, coming from below her, touched her figure here and there into yellow lights, and threw gigantic and misshapen shadows on the walls behind her.

Teresa was trembling. She held one finger to her lips as though enjoining silence, and a hand, outstretched, indicated the door of the dining-room. From the stairs above came the sound of hard breathing. As the men looked at the old woman, she disappeared, melting into the gloom of the staircase.

The duke made a sign to Edward to stay silent where he was, and with his revolver held in readiness, advanced to the door of the room.

It was open a little way only, and but a part of the room was visible. The long table was littered with the remains of a meal, and the cloth at one end had been crumpled and pushed back to clear a space for two men who sat there at cards.

One of them, whose figure showed out darkly against the light of the candelabra, was a personage of massive build, and the duke, taking stock of the bullet-shaped head and thick neck, told himself that here was a customer that would need some handling. The other, his opponent at the game, he saw at a glance was of little account. Old

Pieto had been winning, and a crafty smile of gratified greed flickered over his face as he shuffled the dirty cards.

The watcher by the door noted with some satisfaction that both men applied themselves assiduously to the flagons of wine beside them, in fact, they were neither of them quite sober. As the man whose back was towards him put down his cards he shivered and half turned in his chair with a muttered imprecation upon old women who left doors open.

The duke slipped back into the shadows and raised his weapon and waited. But nothing happened; the man was perhaps too lazy to rise, and was waiting for the return of Teresa.

Edward listened to his companion's whispered instructions carefully. The little old man was to be held at the point of the revolver whilst the duke grappled with the other and stronger man, whose back being turned offered himself as an easy prey.

With a muttered "now," they flung open the door, and with a bound the duke was upon the man at the table, his arm locked around his neck in a vice-like grip. Gradually he bore him backwards, tilting the chair up on its back legs. The ruffian's face was purple, and he made a gurgling noise in his throat. Then the oak of the chair legs cracked, cracked again, and splintered, and the men were on the floor together.

A nimble twist, remarkable in so big a man, and learnt, perhaps, in the bull-ring, put the man on his feet again, and he snatched at a knife on the table. When he turned, the duke was also up, and leaning panting against the wall. The revolver had been knocked from his hand in the struggle, and had fallen neither man knew where.

Keeping his eyes fixed upon his opponent and crouching low, the man with the knife reached out his left hand and took hold of the tablecloth; then, with a swift movement, he dragged it to him, waving it until it was wound round his left forearm. The crockery and glass fell crashing to the floor, and the duke noticed a wine bottle rolling away to the wainscoting, leaving a red trail like blood over the scattered playing cards. But his eyes were quickly back again upon the man, who with his tablecloth-shielded arm was creeping cat-like up to him.

The duke counted himself lost, as, unarmed as he was, he awaited the inevitable spring. He gave one glance at Edward, who was standing over the old manservant, the revolver held waveringly within an inch of the evil face. Povey had not dared take his eyes from his captive; he heard the shuffling of stealthy feet as the men circled round each other, heard one of them kick a dish that was hampering him, sending it crashing against the wall. Then there was the sharp crack of a firearm, and he could stand the suspense no longer.

He turned and saw thin wreaths of smoke floating across the room, and, on the floor, the man whom the duke had attacked half lay, half sat, clutching spasmodically at his knee and swearing horribly. At the door stood Galva. She was very white, and the hand that held the still smoking little pistol was trembling. Edward heard a small pitiful voice. Galva was saying, "In the leg—only—in the leg——"

Then she threw the weapon from her and went over to Edward, and put her arms round his neck.

"Oh, guardy—I've shot a man! Say he's not dead—it was only in the leg—say——" And the girl fell to weeping on his shoulder.

The duke was now standing over Pieto, and was tying the old man's hands with a cord. Teresa bent over the ruffian on the floor, cutting away the breeches from the wound in his leg.

Edward, looking over Galva's shoulder, took in the details of the scene. There was a small pool of blood on the oak boards, and an orange from the table had rolled into it and was dabbled in red.

He saw the duke approach the wounded man, and at his step Teresa looked up. Into her face came a dawning bewilderment, and she gave a little cry.

"Prince Ar——," she whispered. Then the duke had his hand over her mouth. But Edward had heard, and the duke's actions since his arrival in San Pietro were made clear to him.

"This complicates matters considerably," he said below his breath, and went on paternally patting Galva's shoulder.

CHAPTER XXII.

THE HEART OF GALVA

"I think we understood each other in Paris, didn't we, Armand?"

"Yes, dearest, but a definite answer to a definite question is satisfactory; now that you have given me the sweet 'yes,' I will speak to your guardian."

"To-night—speak to him to-night, dear. I know he will be pleased, and," shyly, "if he isn't, I am really afraid that it will make no difference to the 'yes'—or to me."

Galva drew herself away from her lover's embrace.

"He will have something to tell you—about me," she went on rather solemnly; "there he is. Good-night, dearest; I am tired and I want to be alone with my happiness—for I *am* happy to-night, Armand—very happy."

The lips of the lovers met in the shadow of the portico, and when Edward came through the hall he found the duke alone. The two men linked arms and fell to pacing up and down the gravelled space in front of the house. It was not yet eleven and quietude had once more settled down over the Casa Luzo. As they walked, Edward was relating to the duke how he had seen the two prisoners safely disposed of in one of the roomy cellars that ran out under the back courtyard, and had learnt from old Teresa, much to his satisfaction, that it was not likely that Dasso would put in an appearance for some days.

He and Mozara had paid two visits to Casa Luzo since the coming of Galva, but on the last of these the old woman had overheard that, thinking their prisoner perfectly hidden, and the news of her death accepted, Dasso would remain near the Palace waiting for the death of the king. As Edward mentioned the dying monarch he glanced slyly up at the duke's face, paused a moment, then:

"They are saying that your poor uncle can't last long."

At this his companion wheeled round on him.

"So you know my secret?"

"I am not blind, your Highness; you are Armand Enrico Marie, Prince of Alcador, heir-apparent to the throne of San Pietro."

"— —which is the only one of the eleven titles I possess of which I am not proud. It is no honour to claim kinship with King Enrico. But I am glad you know, it saves explanations—I have asked Galva to be my wife."

Edward looked up quickly, then let his gaze rest on the tree tops of the forest.

"Ye gods," he murmured, then felt that the duke was regarding him curiously.

"You are pleased, Mr. Sydney? Galva does not know that it is a throne I am offering her. I will make her a queen, she—what are you looking at, Mr. Sydney?"

Edward drew his eyes back from their contemplation of the tree tops.

"I was thinking," he said slowly.

The duke waited.

"— —Yes, I was thinking," went on Edward, "whether what you have told me—oh, damn it all, you've got to know. Come inside, I think I remember seeing a bottle of wine in there, and I have a story to tell—no, not a word until we have found the bottle and you have heard the story." And the duke, mystified into silence, followed him into the house.

The dining-room still showed some signs of the late struggle, but the *débris* had been in part cleared away, and old Teresa was rubbing vigorously at the blood stain on the oaken floor. She rose from her knees as the men entered, and taking her bucket, slipped from the room. As the door closed behind her the duke broke the silence.

"I really cannot understand the way you have taken my news, Mr. Sydney," he began, a little haughtily, and Edward held up his hand.

"Of course you can't, I can't get the hang of it myself all at once. Sit there, will you? This Chianti is excellent"; then, when the men were seated facing each other across the wood fire—

"You will remember hearing about the tragedy at the Palace at Corbo fifteen years back. I expect you have heard the details over and over again. When the dynasty of the Estratos was all but wiped out——"

"*All but*, Mr. Sydney?"

"That is what I said, prince. The popular belief was that the entire tree of that illustrious house was cut off root and branch, and that all its members perished on that evil night, but it was not so. The Princess Miranda escaped the fate of her parents."

"But the child—a baby—was killed with the queen."

"A child was, but it was not hers. You were speaking to the mother of the dead child only a few hours ago. It is Anna Paluda's little one that lies buried in Corbo Cathedral."

Edward paused impressively, but the duke did not speak. He sat with his dark eyes fixed on the face of the man who was telling the tale.

"That poor woman was foster-mother to the little princess, and the two children were in the night nursery at the time of the tragedy. Queen Elene took up the wrong baby, that's all. It's one of those simple mistakes which mean so much. Anna has sunk her revenge for all these years for the sake of the little girl who was almost as much to her as her own, but her revenge is not dead; some one will pay the price when the princess's affairs are settled."

"And the Princess Miranda, what—what became of her?"

Edward threw a keen look at his listener.

"Anna escaped during the excitement, taking the child with her. A few days later, an American gentleman came across them, living in the deserted hut of some charcoal-burner in the woods. This kind-hearted Yankee, touched by the child's helplessness and the romance of the case, adopted her, smuggled her out of the country, and brought her up to the life of an English lady. Circumstances prevented his taking her back to the States with him, and she and Anna have spent a peaceful life on the Cornish moors until the girl's eighteenth birthday, a few months——"

There came the sound of light singing from the room above them, and with a meaning smile, Edward pointed to the ceiling.

"Her Highness the Princess Miranda seems happy to-night, eh, duke?"

As he spoke Edward leant over with a look of concern, and touched the other on the knee, for the Duc de Choleaux Lasuer was sitting silent, and had buried his head in his hands. "What's all this?" he asked, and noted the anguish that lived in the duke's eyes as he raised his head to answer him.

"It means the loss of everything to me—everything, Mr. Sydney. Throne, position—and a love that is more than my life to me."

"Now, look here, duke: of course the throne is Galva's, there's no getting away from that, but if she loves you and you love her—well—it seems to me that things are fitting in rather neatly."

"Oh, you don't understand. What will the people here say? How will they speak of a man who, having lost a throne, climbs back to it on the shoulders of a woman? The honour of our family is not to be judged by the standard of the devil who is dying back there in Corbo."

The duke had risen as he spoke, but Edward pressed him gently back into his chair.

"I am a plain man, duke, and have lived a plain life—how plain it has been you would never guess. One of these days I will tell you all about the hand I have played in this affair, but not now.

"But in my plain life I have learnt two or three plain facts, and one is that we must take what the good gods give us; they don't, as a rule, hold out their gifts twice. As for this fetish you call honour, what honour is there in spoiling your own life and Galva's too? You say the people will think badly of you. Let them. They will be in the minority, a few kill-joys—remember that all the world loves a lover.

"Yours is a love story that will ring through Europe. Your engagement before either of you knew the high destiny of the other has the true spice of romance, the heart-throb which always fetches the public favour. The Press will fight your battle."

Edward sat down feeling rather surprised at his own eloquence, and drank off a goblet of Chianti. Then he lit a cigar and was silent.

A moment, and the duke turned to him with a sad little smile.

"You put it very nicely, Mr. Sydney. I'll talk to Galva about it in the morning. After all, there are other things to worry about just now.

I think a little action is what I want. You say that Dasso will not be here for a few days?"

Edward nodded.

"He lays great stress on being first in the field when Enrico dies. I don't expect he is ever far from his house for two minutes together. By the way, you know the Palace well, I suppose?"

"Only fairly. I have not been on speaking terms with my uncle for years, except on state occasions when it is policy for me to show up; it's only then that I come to Corbo at all. As a youth I lived in the Palace; my father died when I was eleven. I knew every inch of the building then. It's a rambling old place. Why do you ask?"

"Because I have a plan to suggest. We cannot risk more than one night here, and Galva will be glad to change her surroundings. Among the palace attendants there must be one who can be bribed to smuggle us into the building. It can only be a matter of hours before Enrico dies. Then"—and Edward rubbed his hands together with a crafty smile—"Dasso will find us there to greet him. Won't he be pleased?

"I suggest that we give the wounded ruffian in the cellar money and food. He'll be about again in a day or two. Then Pieto and Teresa, who hate Dasso like poison, will go to their master and tell of the fight and the rescue. They will also say that they overheard us planning to leave the country, that we were heartily sick of San Pietro and all its works. They will, of course, not mention your identity. Anna will join us at the Palace, and my villa will be shut up. This is if you can manage to bribe some attendant whom you know."

The prince thought a moment.

"I fancy it can be managed. I know a way into the grounds. I used it often when I wanted to break bounds. There was Pia, one of the under-gardeners, who was well disposed to me. He ought to be useful if he is still there, as I remember Dasso thrashing him once for spraying him accidentally with a hose. Your Corbian does not forget a thrashing in a hurry. Yes, Pia is our man, I think."

"Very well, then; we will leave here to-morrow afternoon and reach the walls of the grounds by the time it is dark. Then I will slip across Sebastin Park and fetch Anna. After that we will enter by your secret way, and, please Heaven, find your gardener.—We are on the laps of the gods. Now we'll take a watch, two hours each, and don't forget to pray for your uncle—that he may be spared another day."

"Amen to that," said the duke.

"The Princess Miranda begs to inform Enrico Armand, Prince of Alcador, Duc de Choleaux Lasuer, Baron Diaz, Count of the Holy Roman Empire, etc., etc., that she cannot accept the return of anything which she has graciously bestowed upon him—even her freedom."

And saying this, Galva jumped lightly up from the moss-covered boulder upon which she had been sitting, and, smiling mockingly, bowed low before the young man who stood leaning moodily against the straight bole of a pine-tree.

"But, Galva, my honour——"

"Honour, indeed! And does my happiness count for nothing? Does *my* honour not weigh with you? Is it honourable to ask a young girl to show you the treasure-house of her heart and then turn away? Perhaps the wares don›t suit. Perhaps——»

"Galva!"

"No, you must hear me out. Oh, I wish that we were just poor ordinary people, so that we could live only for each other, perhaps away in my lovely Cornwall. But, dear, we aren't just poor ordinary people, and we must go where we are called."

The girl turned and pointed to where the dull crimson of the setting sun shone in the windows of the royal residence.

"There, Armand, is my future home, perched up there above the people whom God has given me to rule. It is for you to make it, for me, a Purgatory or a Paradise—a prison or a home."

She held out her little white hands pathetically and stood there among the trees, her queenly head thrown slightly back, her lips just parted, and with the love-light smiling from under the blue of her lids. And the duke looked at her for a moment—then, with a glad little cry, took her into his arms and kissed her on the lips.

"And now," said the princess as they walked up to a fallen tree trunk which lay half embedded in the undergrowth, "we will sit here and wait for Mr. Sydney—and we won't talk any more nonsense, will we?"

The little party had left Casa Luzo after lunch. Teresa had been instructed to delay the telling of the rescue to Dasso for as long as possible. The wounded man had gratefully accepted the handsome monetary present offered him (especially as Dasso had already paid for his services in advance), and was now making preparations to get back to his native town and the delights of bull-ring society.

The walk through the woods had been a pleasant one to Galva in her new-found happiness and freedom, and her lover had not been able to find the heart to speak the words which he knew would give her pain; in fact, Edward had been gone an hour, leaving them to await his return at the forest edge, before he had summoned up courage to the task. And then had come the battle, and it had lasted exactly ten minutes, and the spoils had been all to Galva. His mind once made up, the duke gave himself with a little sigh to his happiness.

The night came down upon the forest, and still they sat, their fingers entwined, on the fallen tree. The flush had faded from the palace windows, leaving them grey and forbidding, and with sun-down a chill wind had come in from the sea. Behind the lovers the pine trunks showed dimly like vast columns in some ghostly cathedral, and there was no sound save the gentle song of the wind in the branches.

Armand drew the rug they had brought with them closer over both their shoulders, shielding the little head that nestled so confidingly on his breast. When Edward returned with Anna Paluda, the Princess Galva awoke.

The duke rose and stretched his cramped limbs. Edward reached for his hand and shook it.

"Congratulations!" he murmured.

CHAPTER XXIII.

THE PASSING GUN

The particular genius who designed the grounds of the Palace at Corbo was a nephew of the Estratos—a youth of an artistic but somewhat weak intellect and bizarre tastes.

This was in the latter part of the seventeenth century, a period when a wave of decadence had swept over the Court, a time of powder and patches and red-heeled shoes—of mincing courtiers and doubtful gallantries.

Large, level lawns, and flower-bordered walks lay immediately beneath the terrace which ran the length of the building at the back, and beyond and at the sides, the royal horticulturist, with an eye, doubtless, to the doings of the times, had devised cunning shrubberies and fascinating little arbours, the narrow paths twisting here and winding there, a very maze of foliage, paths which had doubtless hampered the movements of many an outraged husband.

Here and there a weather-beaten, moss-patched statue or terminal peeped above the greenery, a nymph with broken features, or a faun, the leer still lingering on his discoloured face. One could imagine him again pricking his goat ears to catch an echo of the sounds he had listened to in those quiet retreats in the days that were gone—the whispered vows, the crunch of high-heeled shoes on the gravel—the oaths and the clash of rapiers.

But Edward's party had more important affairs to hold their attention than the imagining of long-dead romances. They had found without difficulty the entrance into the grounds, and now were making a cautious way over the weed-grown paths.

They had not drawn nearer to the Palace, but had threaded their way through the outer portions of the shrubberies, keeping near to the boundary wall, and coming, after some ten minutes' walk, upon the cottage of the friendly gardener.

The duke stopped as the patch of yellow light from its windows came into view, then quietly led his companions to a stone bench that lay almost hidden in rhododendrons. Here, after seeing the two ladies made comfortable, he left them. The moon had risen and the tangled foliage of the garden was all grey-green and shadow, through which the broken statuary rose, here and there, like pale ghosts of an evil past, looking down on the intruders within their domain of memories.

Armand was away some time, and when he returned he had with him a tall, broad-shouldered man wearing the livery of the keepers of the royal gardens. He stood awkwardly before them, changing from one foot to the other and twisting his green cap nervously in his huge fingers. The duke laid a hand affectionately on the big shoulder.

"These ladies, Pia, and this gentleman, are those of whom we have been speaking." Then turning to Edward, he went on, "I have told this good fellow everything, and although he seems dazed at the whole affair, he is with us heart and soul, as I knew he would be. He has no love for Dasso—and he knows of others who will help us."

At the mention of Dasso's name, the man had looked up, a mask of malignant hate, and the duke, noting it, had given a little smile of satisfaction.

The cottage to which the party was conducted was a roomy building, but of a single storey. Pia's wife at once took charge of Anna and Galva, who were both now showing some signs of weariness. The good woman, noticing this, parted a curtain at the further end of the room, and taking a lamp from a bracket, led the ladies to her bedchamber. The men, left alone, were not slow to take the opportunity of discussing ways and means.

Their plan of action was a simple one. They were to lie hidden where they were until the king was in extremis. Pia, whose daughter was employed as a still-room maid at the Palace, would give them information as to the progress of the royal patient. In the mean time Pia would see that the little staircase which Anna Paluda had used to such good purpose fifteen years before, was free of access, and that the door which gave on to the grounds, and which had fallen into disuse, was cleared of the tangled creepers which he said now all but covered it.

At the first alarm that Enrico's death was imminent, they would make all speed to this door, and hurry up to the room at the top of the stair, the little chamber behind the corridor wall, where ten or twelve people could wait in moderate comfort. Here they would be perfectly secure, and even in the event of the report of the king's condition proving false, they could but retire. At the sound of the first gun announcing the death they would proceed to the king's ante-chamber, there to wait the advent of Dasso. At the least they would be twenty minutes before him.

The ladies did not re-appear but sent their "good-nights" to the men by the old dame, and the duke and Edward were conducted by their host to a barn which lay some ten yards to the rear of the cottage.

Here Pia left them with a stable lantern, telling them that there was no need for them to keep watch. One or other of his sons would be about all night on guard, and nothing could happen without them being made aware of it.

Nothing loath, after their long walk, the two men took off their outer garments, and rolling themselves in the horse blankets provided by Pia, threw themselves upon the pile of yellow straw which littered one end of the barn, and in a few moments they had fallen asleep.

It was bright day when they awoke to find that Pia had entered the barn, bringing with him a jug of steaming coffee and some toasted rolls, to which comforting fare the men devoted themselves whilst they were making their toilet. This completed as well as the lack of razors and other necessaries permitted, they followed their host across the cobbled yard to the great kitchen and living-room of the cottage.

This was a cheerful apartment, whose lime-washed walls, pierced here and there by little red-curtained windows, reflected the glow of the blazing pine logs in the open fire-place. The ceiling was high and pointed, being the entire height of the house, and from the black rafters hung bulky hams and bunches of sweet-smelling herbs. At one end a flight of rough oak steps led up to a little railed gallery that projected out over the fire-place, making a cosy settle, which on winter evenings would accommodate the whole family. In this little gallery were two or three rush-seated chairs, and in a niche in the wall a rather crudely coloured figure of the Virgin.

The morning sunlight shone through the tiny leaded panes of the windows, and glinted on the glass and earthenware laid out on the bare table, spotless as any tablecloth, and made play among the pewter and brass on the great dresser. The cleanliness and order of Dame Pia's room made one imagine oneself in the kitchen of some strict housewife on the Zuyder Zee.

Anna and Galva, refreshed by their night's rest, were in the highest of spirits, which Edward's suggestion that they should not go outside the house hardly lessened. It was so cosy in this sweet-smelling kitchen, and for the moment memories of Cornwall came back to them. They occupied their time well, insisting on giving a helping hand at the housework, much to the embarrassment of the good mistress of the house; and Galva could hardly repress a smile at the expression and the low bow of reverence with which the old woman handed each utensil she had washed to her to wipe.

But the work of one cottage in the hands of three capable women is soon done, and time began to hang heavily on Galva's hands, until, noticing Dame Pia preparing a stew, nothing would satisfy her but that she should try her hand, with what materials were available, at a Cornish pasty. With sleeves rolled up above her dimpled elbows the princess set about her task, the housewife standing dutifully by, her apron twisted between nervous fingers. It was a good pasty, and no doubt the disinclination of the Pia family to eat heartily of it is explained by a little glass case on the dresser which to this day is shown to all visitors, and which shelters the remains of the queen's culinary effort.

Pia went about his work as usual, and Edward mooned rather unhappily about the big room. To the duke this enforced imprisonment was no hardship, and he would sit in the little window-seat watching Galva as she flitted gracefully here and there in the performance of her tasks. No news came to them from the Palace, and as it grew dusk and the lights of Corbo shone in the sky, Edward could stand the inactivity no longer, but disguising his appearance as well as might be, made his way through the Sebastin Park down to the town, choosing the streets that lay near the cathedral in his search for information.

There was, however, nothing to be learnt from the loungers who were taking their coffee and cognac at the little tables of the cafés, and Edward was soon anxious to get back to the cosy comfort of the gardener's cottage. As the chimes in the belfry above him told the hour of nine he rose from the corner of the obscure brasserie where he had been taking his refreshment, and went out into the Cathedral Square.

The air was chilly, and buttoning his coat closely round him he strode out briskly in the direction of the park. He had left the town and entered the Sebastin Gates when he was aware of something unusual in the air. From the direction of the boulevards came the subdued murmur of voices, that intense mumble that speaks of popular excitement. Above the confused sound Edward could make out the shouts of boys crying their papers, and he remembered that it was at nine o'clock that the *Imparcial* made its appearance.

For a moment he stood in indecision. To return to the town meant the loss of half an hour—and surely that rustle of excitement denoted that King Enrico was dead or dying. What a fool he had been to leave the cottage. He might have thought that the absence of news during the day was but the lull before the end, and now here he was out of the game, the success of which he had been playing so hard for.

Pressing his hat firmly on his head, he set off running across the park. After all, he might have been mistaken in imagining that the death had occurred. Surely he would have heard the gun. He knew that the custom was to—

Boom — *m* — *m* — —

The sound echoed and reverberated over the woods and the open spaces round him. Edward slackened his pace, and swore softly to himself. He had come through the secret entrance to the grounds, and now paused a moment and took his bearings.

Then, mending his pace, he ran on, avoiding the cottage, and making direct for the door at the foot of the staircase.

CHAPTER XXIV.

A BULLET IN THE GROUNDS

At the moment when Edward was drinking his cognac in the café in Corbo, Gabriel Dasso was sitting in the library of his house in the old town listening eagerly to a story. Lieutenant Mozara, his spurred riding-boots stretched out to the fire, was telling what had befallen him that afternoon in Alcador.

"It was in a crowd near the little theatre in the Plaza. I only caught a glimpse of him, but I knew the face at once as that of the brute you sent to Casa Luzo. I tried to get near him, but he had evidently seen me, for he slipped into a café. It was a low place, but I followed him. The old proprietor answered my questions with a cunning smile; no one had entered, he told me, and our friend was not among the disreputable crowds that lounged round the tables. There was nothing for it but to hurry on to the Casa Luzo.

"My horse was stabled at the little hotel on the Alcador road, and in under the hour I was interviewing old Pieto, or rather his wife, for the old man was in a state of collapse—and good red wine."

The lieutenant broke off and poured himself out some claret. His host pushed his own glass towards him also, and the two men drank. Then, "Go on," said Dasso, shortly.

"It was a funny story that she had to tell me. She says that yesterday that mysterious Mr. Sydney drove up in a car. With him were the lady companion and three burly ruffians, who, Teresa says, were strangers to her. They seem to have done their work pretty thoroughly, even to the extent of putting a bullet through the leg of your friend from Alcador.

"That was what made me believe the tale, for the man I had seen enter the café was using a crutch. Teresa said that Pieto was asleep at the time, but I expect he was drunk. She says that Galva was bundled into the car, and she overheard Sydney tell her that they were going to Rozana *en route* for England. He was very agitated, she says, and remarked that he was damn sick of San Pietro, and everything and everybody in it.»

"But, Gaspar, you say this was yesterday. Why did not Pieto let me know?"

"They wouldn't allow him to. Two of the men Sydney had brought with him stayed on guard, and it was only — —"

The lieutenant stopped and looked inquiringly at his companion, for through the night-air had come the sound of a gun, muffled, but unmistakable.

Dasso leapt to his feet with an oath.

"Enrico's gone," he said hoarsely, and made for the door. Mozara followed, and in a moment the men, assisted by the under-groom, were saddling Dasso's horse. Gaspar's own mare was on a pillar-rein where he had left her. A moment more and the two men were riding with loose rein up the cobbled street that led to the Palace.

The frightened inhabitants, who were conversing in little groups, scattered to right and left, and windows were opened and heads thrust out as the horsemen clattered past. The Palace gates were open, and dashing through them they pulled up their smoking horses at the great doors.

In the hall the servants, male and female, were crowded, their faces showing inactive stupidity. They fell apart and gave room for Dasso and the lieutenant as they made their way up the wide marble staircase. Reaching the corridor above, they turned to the right in the direction of the death-chamber.

"This is unseemly conduct, Señor Dasso. My uncle is barely dead." Armand was standing before them, a naked blade in his hand.

The intruders fell back.

"Prince Armand—*you* here!»

"It seems so, gentlemen. This is a curious way to pay one's respect to the dead."

Gabriel Dasso stood with bowed head.

"I did not expect— —"

"I did not intend that you should, Señor Dasso. Put up your weapon, Mozara, the guards are within call."

A moment's silence, then Dasso spoke.

"Your Majesty's appearance is timely. The people will be calling for you. They will want to greet the new king."

Armand smiled.

"Perhaps you will lend me the notes of your own speech for the occasion, Dasso; I am rather unprepared. Besides, I do not act for myself, I act for the Queen."

"The Queen?"

"I said 'the Queen,' Señor Dasso. To-night's blunder is not the only one you have made—you made one fifteen years ago when you did your hellish work in this palace."

"You have taken service early, prince, under the banner of this adventuress, this——"

"Señor Dasso," Armand was speaking quietly, "the Queen has ordered that there shall be no bloodshed here to-night. You are forgetting yourself." He called, and four of the royal guard came from a passage behind him.

"Show these gentlemen out. Dasso, I have no royal rank now, and can call you to account for this—by the bye," he added, as the guard closed round the discomfited men, "there will be a special edition of the *Imparcial* to-morrow morning. It will interest you.»

The escort left them at the door and Dasso and Mozara stood undecided on the great steps. Then, leaving their horses, they walked towards the gates. Once out of sight of the building, however, they stopped. Dasso was gnawing at his moustache in impotent fury.

"They told me he was better at seven o'clock. The nurse herself told me. What cursed luck." They walked on again, taking a path that led into the shrubberies. For, perhaps, five minutes they strode on in silence, then the lieutenant halted and caught at his companion's arm.

"Listen!" he said.

From a path close at hand came the sound of running footsteps and the heavy breathing of a spent man. Then round the bend before them emerged the figure of Edward Sydney. With a little laugh Dasso barred his way.

"So," he said.

Edward pulled up short and stared at the wicked faces before him.

"Gentlemen—you will let me—pass?" he gasped.

"I don't think so, Mr. Sydney. Haven't this gentleman and myself, as you English say, a bone to pick with you?"

Dasso smiled grimly as he spoke, a smile which caused a little shiver to pass over Edward and set him looking about him for a possible way of escape.

They had met in one of the narrow paths. On either hand the tall mass of foliage made an impenetrable wall. A few paces away Edward could make out an alley-way which ran at right angles, and he told himself that with luck and a start of a few yards he would stand a good chance of evading capture among the tortuous twists and turns of the shrubbery. In the mean time he must temporize.

"I cannot imagine what your excellency and I can have in common. We have met once—I think at Señor Luazo's, wasn't it?"

"We did meet there, Mr. Sydney, certainly, but it is about the lady who accompanied you here from England that I want to have a word with you."

"You mean Miss Baxendale?"

Dasso nodded.

They had been moving along the path slowly as they were speaking, and Edward noted with satisfaction that now a few feet only separated him from the entrance to the alley. If only he could take the attention of the two men from himself for a moment.—A thought occurred to him.

"Ah, yes—the young lady. If that is so, I think that this will interest you, Señor Dasso."

As he spoke he took from his breast pocket an envelope; it was, in fact, a London tailor's bill and was addressed to him at Belitha Villas, but in the gloom it served its purpose.

Dasso took it and drew out the folded sheet of paper it contained, holding it up to catch the moon-rays which here and there penetrated the leafage surrounding them.

Edward Povey seized the opportunity he had created, and, for the first and last time in his life, he struck a man. The blood surged joyously through his veins and sang a hymn of power in his brain as his fist shot out straight and true, and he felt the knuckles grind into the evil face of Gabriel Dasso. Then with a leap he had gained the dark alley way.

Dasso put a hand to his face and called out to Mozara, and in a moment the lieutenant was giving chase. Edward heard the sound of running footsteps behind him and he mended his pace.

On and on, turning and twisting, ran the poor exhausted little man. In some of the longer paths he would catch a fleeting glimpse over his shoulder of his pursuer, then a sudden plunge to the right or left separated them again.

At last at the end of a more than usually straight run he found himself in the open. To retrace his steps was impossible, already Mozara was but twenty feet from him, the barrel of a revolver shining blue in his hand.

Some hundred yards away the Palace rose, a dark mass against the star-powdered sky, and Edward knew that in the shadow of one of those buttresses lay the little staircase—and safety.

Breathing a hurried prayer for help, he darted across the moon-swept lawns, running unevenly, now upright, now bent nearly double. A shot whined past his ear and he drew in his breath sharply, then another, then—a stinging pain took him in the left shoulder and Edward Povey knew that he had been hit.

Almost at once the acute pain passed and his shoulder grew cold and numb and sticky. He faltered in his stride and all but fell, but the sight of the doorway gave him courage and again he stumbled on.

It took him only two or three minutes to reach it, but to the stricken man it seemed as though he were running for hours. A fog appeared to have risen before his eyes, a reddish fog in which danced and trembled little points of flame—and through the mist he saw the face of Pia, who had been placed to guard the foot of the staircase—felt strong arms supporting him—then with a little sigh drooped into oblivion.

*****

Edward came to his senses to find himself in a dimly lit chamber, with the face of the Princess Galva, white and drawn, bending over him, and her cool hand on his forehead.

Beyond her, in the gloom of the room, were other faces. Anna was there, and the duke, and a strange man whom they addressed as doctor, and who now came forward and took Edward's wrist. The latter could catch here and there a word of what he was saying; the voice seemed to come from a great distance.

"— —unfortunate that it should be this room—locate the bullet— no, again in the morning perhaps—not to be moved—one of the sisters will watch—you can send for me if— —"

Then the faces grew blurred and swayed in circles round the wounded man, and again his senses left him.

CHAPTER XXV.

IN THE DEATH CHAMBER

A dark, silent chamber. A room magnificent and lofty in which the far corners were shrouded in shadowy gloom.

Edward lay in a half consciousness, staring up at the ceiling. It caused him no wonderment that the ceiling was strange to him, and unlike any ceiling he had ever known, or that it should be carved and painted and rich with gilding.

There was a faint, elusive perfume in the air that set him thinking of cathedrals, and from somewhere near him there came a droning monotone.

He felt no definite pain now, only a sensation of lassitude and detachment. There was a strange tightness in the region of his heart and he felt a little cold. Turning his head he tried to rise upon his elbow, but a sharp pain took him in the shoulder as he moved, and he was glad to sink back again upon the pillow.

The movement, however, slight as it had been, had left him in a position from which he could get a better view of his surroundings, and as he took these in he gave a little gasp and felt the beads of moisture pricking out upon his forehead.

In the centre of the room there was a bed, the four posts of which, richly carved, upheld a fluted canopy of dull red silk from which depended heavy curtains looped up with tasselled cords. Upon the panel above the pillow an escutcheon was blazoned out in dull gold.

Edward closed his eyes for a moment before he could make up his mind to let them rest on the figure which he knew he would see lying beneath the crimson canopy. He asked himself what could have been the cause of his, Edward Povey's, presence in the death chamber of the king of San Pietro. Then he opened his eyes and looked.

Enrico was lying stiff in the centre of the bed, the sharp points of his knees and feet showing rigidly through the white sheet which covered his body. The thin hands were folded peacefully upon the breast, and between the stiffening fingers had been thrust a crucifix of ebony, bearing a silver image of the Christ. Below the hands, too, Edward noticed that some one had placed a single bloom, a rose. The little flower stood out eloquently among the sombre pageantry of death, "all the purer for its oneness," and he wondered idly whether it spoke of at least one who had truly sorrowed at the passing of the king, at one real regret.

On the bed, at the feet of the dead monarch, were two cushions on which were pinned the several orders and medals which had belonged to Enrico; his sword, too, lay between them, together with his plumed hat and his field-marshal's staff.

On either side of the bed there knelt a Sister of Mercy, and it was the monotone of their prayers that Edward had heard when he first awoke. In an alcove by the great carved fire-place a thin spiral of scented smoke rose from a censer. Four tall candles in silver holders made the space round the body an oasis of light, and in the cavern of shadow beyond loomed the strange shapes of massive furniture, and the dull gleam of mirrors. The heavy curtains had been drawn across the windows, and there was no sound but the murmur of the women at prayer and the occasional fall of a cinder on the stone flags of the hearth.

The scene was eerie in the extreme, and Edward gazed in fascinated interest at the rigid figure on the bed. Enrico had been a handsome man in life, and with the passing of his evil soul his earthly dignity of aspect had increased. The head was lying well back and showed the noble sweep of the brow and the clean-cut profile of the high-bridged nose. A full beard, raven black and threaded here and there with grey, rested spread out like a pall upon his breast and reached to the clasped hands. Upon the sunken wax-like cheeks the firelight flickered and played ghastly shadow tricks in the hollows of the deep-set eyes.

One of the nuns rose silently from her knees to attend to a candle at the head of the bed which had been guttering in a little draught that had found its way into the still room. As the woman turned to resume her prayers she saw that Edward, upon his pile of rugs in the corner, was awake, and she came with noiseless steps over to him. She laid a cool hand upon his brow and spoke to him in a whisper.

"You are not to talk, señor; I have orders to fetch the Queen to you when you awoke."

"The Queen!—you call her that already! But she will be asleep, she——" He ceased speaking as the white hand was pressed over his lips, and he watched the sister as she glided noiselessly to a door that was concealed behind a curtain near him.

In a few moments she had returned, and behind her, Edward saw Galva, and a smile lit up his rather tired-looking eyes as she crept and knelt down by the side of the made-up couch.

Very adorable looked the young Queen of San Pietro as she bent her lovely head over Edward Povey. Her hair, parted in the centre, fell over her shoulders in two long plaits, showing their dark richness against the steel blue of the wrapper the girl had put on. Her face was a little pale and there were dusky rings showing under the eyes—eyes which still held a suspicion of tears.

The nun who had fetched her crossed the room and touched her fellow watcher on the arm, and together they left the room.

When they were alone Galva bent lower over towards Edward and he put out his hands and took her little ones between them, and as he did so something warm fell upon them.

"Why, Galva—what's all this—tears? Why——"

"Oh, guardy, you are hurt—and I can't bear it. I would never forgive myself—never, if anything were to happen to you. It is my fault—it——"

"I don't know, Galva, whether I'm badly hurt or not—sometimes I think I am. I don't feel much pain now—but there is a tightness here. Why was I put in this room, into the presence of death? Enrico in all his glory is hardly the best of company for an invalid." And he smiled a little.

"It was the doctor, guardy, the man who had been attending the king. He had you brought here as it was nearest, and he won't let them move you. He tried to find the bullet, but he couldn't. He is coming again in the morning. Who shot you, guardy?"

"Never mind that now, dear. I want to ask you something. I want you to tell me if— —if— —I have been of use to you, if I have helped ever so little to put you where you are now—to make you Queen of San Pietro."

Galva raised her head.

"Why, Mr. Sydney, what a strange question—of course— —"

"Not so strange, dear, not so strange. Don't call me Mr. Sydney, just Edward. And so I have really helped a little? I'm glad. I'm—do you know, Galva, that I have always thought that in this life we are given our chance to combat the evil we do with good, to balance our account, as it were; that for every sin we commit, every wrong we do, we are given a whitewash brush, to use if we will."

"I think so too, guardy—but you have done no wrong. I won't believe any evil of you—you are all that is noble and good."

Edward shook his head.

"But you don't know everything, there are one or two little things which one of these days, when I am better, I will explain to you. Now go to bed, dear; this wrapper of yours is as thin as paper. In the morning I will explain—yes, explain. Good-night. Oh, by the bye, that is your rose, I expect, isn't it?" and he pointed to the bed, and Galva nodded. "I thought so, you little saint; I don't know any one else who would have put it there. Now run away, dear—-in the morning I will explain."

The girl rose and leant over the wounded man.

"Good-night, guardy dear, and God bless you," she said, and kissed him on the lips.

She turned at the door and sent him a little smile, and as she went from sight behind the curtain, a sense of desolation came over Edward Povey.

He thought it would be good to die like this—and perhaps it were better that there should be no explanation. He had taken on the mission of a man who was unable to act for himself, and he had carried it to a successful issue. All was right with the world, and he told himself that his own account was with God in His heaven.

He became mildly delirious and asked himself what more could he desire of the Romance he craved, than to pass out of life here in this chamber which might have been lifted bodily from a classic of the Middle Ages? What fitter surroundings than the tall sombre candlesticks, the praying women, the silence, and the shrouded figure on the bed? He turned his eyes to Enrico and felt a strange sense of companionship.

The pain in his chest seemed easier now, and the spasms were becoming less frequent. He lay between sleeping and waking, in a delicious state of ease. He thought tenderly of Charlotte, and wondered if she would miss him very much if she were never to see him any more.

There had been little love, little real love, between them for the past few years, but in his light-headedness Edward thought of her as he saw her that day years ago, decked out in the tawdry white finery of their wedding morning, trembling beside him at the altar of the shabby little Barnsbury church. He called to mind the girlish, shrinking figure standing on the threshold of life, and he remembered that there were tears shining through the cheap little net veil.

Then he went on through the years, through the hopefulness of it all, and the disappointments, through the troubled waters with their sun-kissed moments, to the dull tinged sea of matrimonial failure. He could not really blame Charlotte; her lot had been perhaps a harder one than his, after all.

Even the journey to and from the City, the noisy companionship of the second-class smoker, the life of the gloomy counting-house, the snack of lunch followed by the grateful pipe smoked on the sunny side of Gracechurch Street—these had all been his, and he knew now how they had all helped him to endure those years in the little villa at Brixton.

He wondered idly why God had not sent them any children. Little ones were so necessary to life. Charlotte and he would never have drifted apart if the wondering eyes of a child had been there to see— if there had been tiny roseleaf hands to hold them to each other. It would all have been so different then.

The blind at one of the windows had become disarranged, and through the aperture Edward saw the first sweet flush of the dawning. It was only a little glimpse, but he could see an inch or two of the horizon. Above the silver edge of a bank of stormy clouds that lay low over the sea, the coming day had barred the sky with green and gold and shell pink and glory. Gradually the light in the room increased, and the candles grew ghostlike, and the shadows lifted unexpectedly from the corners.

The two nuns had re-entered the room, and one of them crept softly over to his couch and gazed down at the white face. Then she tiptoed back and touched her companion on the arm.

"We will whisper our prayers, sister; our little friend is in a delicious sleep. He'll do now. We must think of the living before the dead."

CHAPTER XXVI.

THE FUGITIVE

In dynasties, as in politics, the pendulum pursues its immutable law. Those who, or whose immediate ancestors, had applauded the tragedy of fifteen years ago, were now to be seen in the very forefront of the rejoicings at the fair Estrato who had come out of the blue to rule over them.

The editor of the *Imparcial* had at last had his great chance, and the Marinoni he had purchased second-hand from a Madrid printing office was working overtime. For edition after edition he drove home the praises of the rising stars of San Pietro. With the true journalistic spirit he had seized on the high lights of the romance, points which he knew would delight the gossip-loving patrons of his sheet, and the café loungers on the promenade of Corbo were regaled with stories of the love of Galva and Armand, which, if not strictly true, were at least richly garnished with the roses of romance and were well worth the reading.

As a counterblast, *El Dia* had appeared the morning following the death of the king, with a heavy, wordy, black-bordered leading article in which the influence of Spain was barely disguised. It had pointed out to the inhabitants of San Pietro that they would do well to move warily in the crisis now before them, and that, at least, they should stay the celebrations of joy until after the vault in Corbo Cathedral had closed over the remains of the late king, whose small virtues they unearthed and glorified.

But your Corbian is not given to moving warily, and neither can he pretend to a sorrow he does not feel. It is small wonder, therefore, that the gala colours of rejoicing should outweigh the trappings of woe with which a few axe-grinding friends of the late monarch bedecked their sorrowing persons.

From an attic window high up in a small and dirty hotel facing the Cathedral Square, and well shielded by the faded and torn curtains, a man had sat for days watching the animated scenes beneath him. He sat with his chin moodily resting in his hand, in his eyes the haunted look of a man who is hard pressed.

*****

Gabriel Dasso and the lieutenant had, after the encounter with Edward Povey in the shrubbery of the palace grounds, made their way to the house in the old town. The ex-dictator did not consider all was lost until Spain had had her say in the matter; he relied, too, on the army, a hope which would have been fully justified had he had only Prince Armand as an opponent.

But he well knew the natures of the gay-hearted youths who held commission in the San Pietran army, and, knowing this, he sighed, and a vision of a lovely face rose up before him, a face in which the dark eyes shone serenely and fearless, and luminous with fascination. He felt that only too readily would the swords fly from their scabbards to do service for Queen Miranda.

The men let themselves into the house in the old town and made their way to the dining-room. Dasso went over and drew the heavy curtains across the windows. There was wine on the table and he drank greedily. Mozara was standing dejectedly before the fire, jabbing viciously at the logs with his heel. The sight of the spur reminded him of something, and he gave a hard little laugh.

"We might have brought away our horses, Gabriel—we may need them," he said meaningly.

"Pshaw, we'll win yet." But Dasso's tone was not hopeful as he said it, and the hand that held the wineglass trembled a little, which was not usual with the hand of the ex-dictator.

"What! You have been busy with your schemes, Dasso; you have not noticed the eyes of the Queen, perhaps. Win!"—and the lieutenant snapped his fingers—"impossible."

Gabriel Dasso leant over the table and he spoke in a low whisper. Perhaps it was the wine that caused the huskiness to come into his voice.

"I saw eyes, Gaspar, like those *fifteen years ago*—and I won then. What is to prevent our doing *now* what we did *then*?"

He remained silent for a moment, his eyes never leaving Mozara's face.

"——*now*, what we did *then*," he repeated; "the people know nothing of this girl, and before the story can leak out it will be all over. I can get the captains from the barracks, Luaz and Pinto, and—oh, they'll all come with me. The girl shall not be mentioned; they will think there is only Armand there, and you know what they think of him. But it must be now; I will not count on their help when once they have seen her. I myself will find the girl and deal with her as I dealt with her moth——"

With an oath the lieutenant started forward; the glass he had been holding crashed to the floor, and his breath came in little painful gasps.

"You devil—you—Oh, I knew the downward path was broad, I did not think it was so short. Only a few months since that evil day when I fell under your thumb. Before the night of the cards I had been no worse than the others, now—— What's that, Dasso?"

The lieutenant had broken off suddenly and stood in the attitude of listening, his face grey and set. For a moment there was a strained silence in the room, then there came to the ears of the men a confused distant murmur. Dasso reached out a hand and extinguished the lamp.

Cautiously the two men, brought together now by a common danger, moved to the window; the flicker of the logs in the grate lit up the fear on their faces. Gabriel drew the blind aside for about an inch and stood waiting.

All seemed quiet again now, and the men told themselves that they had heard some drunken roysterers on their way home from the Casino. After a few moments they returned to the fire. There was a sneer on Dasso's face as he turned to the younger man and took up the quarrel where it had been interrupted.

"So you prefer to remain here and be disgraced, eh? My plan is the only one left and to-night is the only time for the doing. If we succeed Spain will gloss over the affair; if we fail——"

"Stop, Gabriel, I won't listen to you, and I'll do no more of your hellish work. A few mouths ago my life was at least decent. I'll have no dealings with you after what you have said. I can only thank God that I was with you in this, else that poor girl would have had no mercy shown her and would now be dead. Perhaps that will atone a little when I meet my Maker. I'll expose you, Dasso—you—you murderer."

The spring that Dasso made took the lieutenant unawares and bore him heavily to the ground, his head striking one of the carved iron firedogs as he went down with a dull crash, and he lay still where he had fallen. The face of the elder man was livid with passion.

"You'll expose me, eh? Murderer, eh? Many have thought that, but no one has called me it to my face." The fingers were tightening round the throat of the unconscious officer.

"When—you—meet—your—Maker, you said. That will be to-night, my friend." He pressed more heavily, leaning his weight full upon the body.

And when all was over and the form beneath him no longer made any movement or sound, he stood up. There were great beads of moisture on his face, and the decanter clinked pitifully against the glass as he poured out more wine.

He took the cloth from the long sideboard and dropped it over the face of the man on the floor.

Now the sound that they had heard came to him again in little bursts, and he walked unsteadily to the window. Pieces of the glass dropped by Mozara crunched under his heel.

The lamp had not been relit, and the murderer was able to see clearly into the moon-bathed street. The Three Lilies was in darkness— evidently the sound had not come from that quarter.

Again. This time it was more pronounced, and Dasso could make out a dark patch, dotted with lantern light, moving towards the house from the direction of the town. As the murmur grew more distinct, the watching man could make out a word here and there; they were calling his name, and the epithets attached to it were not flattering.

Dasso left the window, and crossing to the fire peered into the steel face of the clock that stood in the centre of the mantelshelf. Then in the half light he went over to the little safe embedded in the wall.

He unlocked it with trembling fingers and took from it package after package of papers and carried them over to the fire, and placing them on the seat of a chair began his task of sorting. Some were put upon the burning logs without a second glance; others, including a large roll of paper money, he placed in the breast pocket of his coat.

There were other documents, too, which caused a furrow to take shape between the evil brows, and which were held to the glow and read through from their first word to their last before they were finally pocketed or sent to swell the growing pile of grey ash on the smouldering logs.

Only once did the man look towards the thing that lay still and sinister on the great bearskin rug not two feet from where he knelt. This was when he picked up the envelope containing the hand at cards which had been the downfall of the man who now was dead.

Dasso held the package for a moment in his hand, the custodian of a dead man's honour. He seemed to be debating whether Mozara could in any way further serve him. Then as the noise outside grew louder he thrust the envelope between the bars and rose to his feet. Now there came a knocking at the great oaken door, and Dasso heard his name called by angry voices. He knew why the mob had come seeking him, and he knew the temperament of the Corbians, that they were creatures in whom civilization and barbarism were separated by the faintest of lines, and who knew no restraint or reason once their passions were aroused.

A stone hurtled through the window-pane and checked by the blind fell down with a clatter on to the polished floor and rolled almost to his feet. For the first time Dasso showed signs of haste.

He made his way from the room and through many passages to the servants quarters at the back, taking, as he ran, from a peg in the lower hall, a wide-brimmed hat and a common brown cloak which had belonged to old Pieto.

There came a crashing and splintering from the front of the house, and the man told himself that the stout oak had given at last. He opened a door beside the great dresser shutting it behind him and shooting home the heavy metal bolts. He descended a short flight of steps that lay there, and which led down to the cellars of the old mansion. At the foot he waited, and feeling out with his hands he found and lit a horn lantern.

Through cellar after cellar he made his tortuous way, past bins and racks of wine, between casks and cases stacked high to the groined roof. The air was thick and musty and great rats scampered away at the approach of the flickering yellow light and the hurried footsteps.

Then the air grew cooler, and Dasso stopped and, raising his lantern, searched the walls round him. A few stone steps led up to an opening, through which with stooping shoulders the man passed. Here he was in a tunnel, a narrow tube, that rose gradually until the fugitive could feel the cool airs of the night upon his face, and he found himself in front of an iron gateway. He took from the pocket of his coat a key, and after a few attempts the gate was thrust open, tearing its way through the mass of vegetation with which the iron-work and hinges were choked, and Dasso stood in the moonlight of the vegetable garden of his house. A thick belt of trees separated him from the building itself, and in the distance he heard the cries of the mob who had now gained an entrance. He clenched his fists and turned away. As he did so, through the trees a light splashed redly, then another—and another, and the man knew that they had set fire to the building.

A curse spluttered out between his teeth as, dropping the lantern into a water butt that stood at hand, he started to run along the path that led away from the house.

For perhaps a hundred yards he ran, the path leading between beds of celery and fruit bushes. The moonlight cut the garden up into sharp black-green shadows, which were illuminated now and again by flashes of light from the burning house behind him.

At the foot of the garden a high wall, spiked with broken glass, barred his way, and turning to the left he ran along at its base till he came to a door, bolted and barred. In a few moments he had this open, and was out in a small lane that ran behind the house.

Following this he emerged into a broader road, and again into the main street in which stood what was left of his home. Here, disguised as he was, he was safe, and he stood in a doorway and looked up towards the burning house.

The fire had by now obtained a firm hold, and the old worm-eaten woodwork was blazing vividly. Silhouetted against the glow were the dark figures of the incendiaries, like imps of the netherworld, leaping and howling in drunken joy, and Dasso guessed, and rightly, that some of the choice vintages it had been his whim to lay down had fallen into their unappreciative hands.

Higher and higher leaped the flames, casting a glow as of burnished copper on the dark violet of the sky. Higher, too, rose the voices of the mob; they were singing now a song of the Estratos, and one which had not been heard in the streets of Corbo for many a long day.

For perhaps half-an-hour the man stood in the doorway watching the downfall of his home and of his hopes. Then, drawing his cloak round him and pulling his hat well over his face, he made his way to the Cathedral Square.

He had to stop many times on the way to slip into the friendly shadow of some porch. Late as it was, the town seemed *en fête* on this night when their king lay dead in the Palace. The cafés were open and crowded with revellers, and bands of youths rushed madly past the homeless man, attracted by that beacon shining in the sky which promised devilment and plunder. It took Dasso, perhaps, half-an-hour before he emerged into the comparative quiet of the square facing the Cathedral.

At the side door of a dirty little hotel he stopped and rapped. The door was opened by the landlord himself, an evil-looking ruffian, who held the candle he carried up high to see who it was who came knocking at this late hour. Dasso took off his hat. The innkeeper fell back.

"Señor Dasso—why, what brings——"

"Don't stand there talking, fool, I'm coming in." He smiled cruelly. "You won't refuse a lodging to me, Gambi, surely."

The old man drew aside, and the hand holding the candle trembled. The visitor made his way into the kitchen of the hotel.

For a fortnight now the man had been sitting almost incessantly at the window looking down into the Cathedral Square. He had seen many happenings—the State procession of the new King and Queen when they attended Mass, the shouts of the multitude, and the smiles of the royal beauty in the carriage.

One night, too, a huge bonfire had been lighted in the square, and an effigy, whom he had no difficulty in recognizing, had been burnt to the accompaniment of drunken jeers and savage howls of execration.

The innkeeper, whose many misdeeds made him loath to offend his unwelcome guest, to whom they were well known, told him that the people were searching high and low for him, and that they had now come to the conclusion that he had left the island.

"In another week or two, Gambi, when my beard has grown more, their conclusion will be justified," Dasso had remarked, and the innkeeper had been very relieved indeed to hear it.

CHAPTER XXVII.

THE IMPOSTOR

The sun newly sunk behind the Yeldo Hills had stained the sky with rose and amber, and it was very peaceful in the darkening grounds of the Palace of Corbo.

The woods were alive with the evening songs of the birds, and a light wind that blew in from the sea brought with it the chimes from the Cathedral belfry. The shrubberies loomed big in the violet twilight and afar out the sea lay placid, steel-blue and mysterious.

Edward Povey, surveying the scene from the comfort of a bath-chair, was putting to himself a few pertinent and very necessary questions. Some lines which he had heard years back came into his mind, he couldn't remember them exactly, but they had to do with what the devil would do when he was sick.

Amongst other thoughts which crowded into the brain of Mr. Povey were the warm feelings he had experienced towards Charlotte when, as he thought, he lay dying in Enrico's death chamber, and he told himself that they were very right thoughts to have.

He remembered also the events of the past few months, Galva's unremitting care and tenderness to him during the period of his convalescence. The thought that the time had now come when his part in her affairs was done was a very bitter one, but as day followed day the feeling that he was an impostor grew stronger. He had long thought that he must get away from it all. Every kind word, every smile was a stab to him. To explain matters now would do no good, spoiling as it would Galva's happiness. He hated, too, to think of her eyes regarding him in any other way but with admiration, the thought of the disgust that might show in her face unnerved him. He felt very thankful that his fears of death had been premature, and that he had been spared to witness the reception by the Corbians of their new Queen, but, at the same time, the grim visitor would at least have put him out of his predicament.

His recovery had not been rapid enough to allow of his attending the festivities of the Coronation, which had taken place with much pomp and circumstance a few weeks after Enrico had been laid in the Cathedral. The kindly doctor, however, had permitted the invalid's couch to be wheeled out on to one of the balconies of his room.

From there he had seen the procession leave the palace, had noted the enthusiasm of the holiday crowd, and, best of all, had seen Galva turn in her carriage and wave her bouquet of orchids at his balcony. Then the cavalcade, winding like a gaily coloured stream of ribbon, had been swallowed up in the twistings and turnings of the old town, and Povey, lying there in the genial afternoon sunshine, had been left to imagine the rest.

By the aid of his field glasses he had seen the bunting and banners fluttering bravely on the buildings in the town, which lay spread out beneath him shining like a jeweller's tray of gems in the sun-rays. He had seen the yachts in the bay gay with little flags. He had heard, too, the bells pealing joyously from the tall belfry of the Cathedral, the firing of the guns on the fort, and the distant murmur of the people cheering their Queen.

He had said a little prayer for everybody and had fallen asleep there on the flower-decked balcony. When he awoke he was again in his room and the candles were being lit.

The Queen of San Pietro stood there before him flushed with her happiness and resplendent in her finery of state. Her little head was thrown slightly back and she appeared taller than she really was in the sweeping mantle of crimson and ermine which fell from her shoulders and spread out on the carpet behind her. As she noted the wondering admiration on Edward's face she gave him a delightful little smile.

"A right down, regular, Royal Queen," she quoted gaily as she dropped an elegant curtsey. "Oh, guardy dear, it's been splendid— just splendid—nothing but sun and cheers and flowers—and joy."

She turned to her husband who was standing a little behind her, for the ceremonies in the Cathedral had been twofold that day, and the Archbishop who had placed the crown on the little head, had, in the little private chapel, placed a circlet of gold also on the Queen's finger.

"I didn't see a single house, Armand," she ran on, "that was not flying a flag. And to think that we owe all this to guardy here. If he had died, and we really thought he was going to, didn't we? there would have been no joy, then, only — —"

She had leant over and kissed him and Armand had taken his hand and gripped it hard. Was it any wonder that the explanation that had hovered so long on Edward's lips retired from the unequal contest?

And now as he sat in his bath-chair he remembered all these things, and sighed regretfully as he told himself that there was only one way left for him in honour to take. It was time for him to leave the stage, to take off the motley, for he had no part in the next act of the drama.

The attendant, who in the gorgeous Estrato livery was slowly propelling the chair, pulled up rather suddenly, as, turning into one of the alley-ways which led back to the palace he came in sight of the figure of a woman. Anna Paluda turned at the sound of the wheels on the gravel, and Edward saw that she thrust a paper hurriedly into the black silk reticule hanging by a cord from her waist. Her manner, too, as she came towards him, was, he thought, a little strained. Evidently Madame Anna Paluda had been taken somewhat unawares.

For a little while, after greeting Edward, she walked on beside the bath-chair, speaking of commonplaces, on subjects ranging from the politics (such as they were) of San Pietro to the evening light shining in the western windows of the palace. Then a sudden thought came to the man in the chair and he turned to the lady by his side.

"This chair is quite light, Anna; do you think you could — or better still, I will walk the rest of the distance, it isn't far."

"You'll do nothing of the sort. I know you *can* walk, but you will find the air chilly after all those rugs.» She turned to the attendant, «You can go, Juan — I will attend to Mr. Sydney."

With a bow the man left them, and Anna, taking the handle, leant over to the occupant of the chair.

"You wanted to say something to me?"

A moment's final hesitation, then Edward took the plunge.

"Yes, Anna, I wanted to tell you that I intend leaving Corbo for England as soon as the doctor will let me. My business, you know— I've been away from it long enough."

"But you will come back, Mr. Sydney?"

"Oh yes—that is, I——Oh, I'm sure to come back—yes—sure— to—come—back."

Had Edward been facing Anna as he spoke he would have noticed a curious light creep into the black eyes, as though something had occurred suddenly to her. One hand involuntarily left the handle of the chair and caressed the black silk reticule. As she felt the paper under her fingers she smiled.

"But—some one will have to go with you—you have had an illness—it isn't safe, is it, for you to travel alone?"

"Tut, tut, Anna, I'm fit as a cello. Why, I walked twice round the palace this morning; besides, I'm not going to-morrow." Now that his departure had been decided on, and he had burnt his boats, he felt disposed to allow himself the luxury of delay. "It may be a month before I really go," he added.

Again Edward would have seen a look come into Anna's eyes— disappointment this time, unmistakable disappointment at his last words.

But the woman said nothing, and before Edward spoke again the chair had reached the doorway of the palace and footmen were assisting him to alight.

Anna accompanied him up the broad staircase, until he reached the corridor on which his apartment was situated, then she turned and made her way swiftly to her own room. Entering, she locked the door and crossed to the large wardrobe which took up one side of the apartment wall. From beneath some clothes in a drawer she lifted her leather jewel case, and carrying it over to the dressing-table lit the candles which stood on either side of the draped mirror. She selected a tiny key from the bunch at her waist and, opening the case, took out a box, a little cardboard box, which had once contained chocolates. The lid was broken here and there, and had been carefully pasted together with scraps of plaster paper. Anna removed the cover carefully and tenderly, and leant her head in her hands and gazed down at what lay therein.

A baby shoe of white kid, soiled and still showing the shape of tiny toes, a bunch of faded ribbon, a little armless doll with staring beady eyes; and, most pathetic of all, two or three of the original chocolates the box had held—hard and colourless.

The woman raised her head and looked at herself in the mirror. She had not been crying, for her eyes were quite dry, but into them had come a look of determination, of a set purpose in which tears had no place and tenderness no part. She looked again at the articles in the box.

"A little while—not long now," she murmured, "then, perhaps I may weep."

Silently she put away the baby relics back into the wardrobe drawer. Then from the reticule she took the letter she had been reading when Edward had come upon her in the grounds. She smoothed out the creases and held it to the light on the dressing-table. It was headed from the offices of *The Imparcial*, and read—

"MADAM,

"Acting under your instructions, I have caused inquiries to be made by my correspondents in Paris, London and Vienna. The man Dasso, who disappeared so suddenly from Corbo, had covered his traces so well that it was not until now that we have lit upon a clue of any sort.

"My Paris correspondent in the Rue Scribe, M. Dupine, has been watching, as you suggested, the places of entertainment and the restaurants on the boulevards. Your idea that our man would appear sooner or later at one or the other of these was quite correct. M. Dupine came face to face with him in the lounge of the Folies Bergere.

"Curiously enough, Dasso seemed to scent danger, for he left hurriedly, but Dupine succeeded in following him. He tells me he (Dupine) was reading a copy of my paper at the time he saw Dasso, and attributes the latter's flight to that fact.

"Dasso left the Gare St. Lazare the next morning, travelling to Dieppe, and so across the Channel.

"Dupine, being now known by sight to Dasso, wisely refrained from following him on to the boat, where he would have certainly been *observed, but wired comprehensively to a confrere in Brighton to motor over to Newhaven and take up the chase.*

"I have heard only this morning that this gentleman has been successful, and that Dasso is now staying in unpretentious lodgings in Bloomsbury, No. 9, Dorrington Street.

"Having thus, madam, followed out your wishes, I have only to assure you that my information will be kept secret until such time as you give consent for publication. I thank you for your promise that I shall have first and exclusive news of eventualities, and beg to assure you of my devoted services.

"I am, madam,
"Yours obediently,
ALFONSO PINZATO
"(Editor)."

For a long time the excuse that she would have to make to Galva before she could leave the island had been worrying Anna. She thought of Edward as she folded the letter and put it away.

"Yes, some one must travel with him—Galva would never let him go alone. Edward Sydney, the sooner you are able to travel the better I shall be pleased."

CHAPTER XXVIII.

EDWARD DEPARTS

Edward's convalescence progressed apace when once his course of action was decided upon. It had been a severe blow to Galva's happiness that she was so soon to lose the little friend whom she had come to love—a blow that was not softened by Anna's asking permission to accompany him.

That her guardian was not sufficiently well to travel alone, however, made the woman's request a perfectly natural one, and when at last Edward and his self-appointed nurse, the farewells over, entered the carriage that was to convey them to the dock-side, the Queen met the situation bravely.

It was not until, from an upper window of the palace, she had seen the boat dip below the horizon, that the fall extent of her loss came home to her. She remembered, with a little catch at the heart, that Edward, whilst seeming to answer her many questions as to his return, had really most successfully evaded them.

Anna she was certain of. The new rulers of San Pietro had decided that in a month or so they would take a holiday, a little trip in which for a week or two they would become again just ordinary people. As the Duke and Duchess Armand de Choleaux Lasuer they would renew their acquaintance with the French capital and the long, straight motor roads, and afterwards, as Mr. and Mrs. Baxendale, they would take up their abode at the little Cornish cottage on the purple moors which the girl, in secret, so longed to see again.

There they were to rejoin Anna, who would have all in readiness for them, and she looked forward with delight to the time when she could wander at evening over the hills above Tremoor, watching the lighthouses flash their warnings out over the sea and the gulls circle and scream above the rocky cliffs and the restless Atlantic. It would be a real honeymoon. Armand had never been in the "Delectable Duchy," and Galva was never tired of thinking of the things she could show him in the glorious land where her girlhood had been spent so happily.

The court they held at Corbo was unpretentious in the extreme, and after the coronation and the state receptions attendant thereon, life at the palace had quieted down to a peaceful existence untrammelled by the ceremonies which appertained to larger and more important kingdoms.

The girl-queen often wondered what it would have been like had she been alone. With Armand it was just as though they were living in a glorious country home; they drove out unattended, and took motor rides to one or other of their houses in the other parts of the island with as much privacy as they had run out to Fontainebleau in the days when they had first met.

The business pertaining to the State of San Pietro was slight, and Señor Luazo, who had been elevated to the post of Chancellor, proved himself invaluable. Galva saw to it that the abuses which had sprung into being under the administration of King Enrico were remedied. Trade improved, visitors, attracted by the royal love story, came in increased numbers. The Corbians at heart were a lazy, contented people, and if only left alone the little toy kingdom really seemed to rule itself.

The boat train had drawn up at Victoria a few minutes after seven o'clock, and still Edward and Anna were sitting in one of the cushioned alcoves of the station buffet drinking coffee.

They each knew that their journey, in company, had come to an end, and they mutually avoided the subject of separation. Each felt that the address to which he or she were going would be expected by the other, and each was unwilling to give it. And so they sat and talked of many things until the clock pointed to nine o'clock. Then Anna rose and held out her hand.

"Well—good-bye for the present, Mr. Sydney," she said nervously, "I can write to you—where?"

"Oh, yes—Anna—good-bye. I—I'm a little uncertain as to my movements for the next few days. I—oh, by the bye, where are you staying?"

Anna Paluda bent down and took up her jewel case and handbag.

"Well, Mr. Sydney—I'm like you—uncertain. I have an aunt—but she may be away. Suppose we communicate in the agony column of the *Morning Post*—that will be romantic, won't it?" with a little smile.

"Er—yes—just the very thing. E.S. to A.P.—well, good-bye again. I'll get you a cab."

Under the glass-covered yard Edward handed Anna into a taxi which had just driven up and deposited a passenger. He tried to catch the address the woman whispered to the driver, but she spoke very low and he was unsuccessful.

He stood on the curb with his hat in his hand, smiling his farewells until the cab had passed through the gates. Then he gave a little sigh and made his way in the direction of the Park.

"So that is all," he murmured sadly to himself. "God's in His heaven, Galva's on her throne, all's right with the world—and Edward Povey's little flutter is over."

He turned slowly through the gates, and stood looking at the façade of Buckingham Palace. And as he gazed at the rows of windows and at the railed courtyard, with the sentries, his thoughts turned to another palace, a palace under a blue sky and which overlooked a glittering jewel city in the sun-kissed waters of a southern sea.

"God bless *my* little Queen,» he said, and turned and walked to where the lights of Piccadilly were shining in the sky.

He wandered aimlessly along among the evening throng of pleasure seekers. He felt lost, he seemed to have forgotten that London existed. He turned into the Monico and drank a whisky and soda, and as he came out he saw a green 'bus drawing up at the curb outside the Pavilion music hall. The conductor was shouting—"Russell Square, King's Cross."

"Do you pass Abbot's Hotel?" Edward asked.

"Just near it, sir."

And Edward, giving himself no time for second thoughts, mounted to the top.

CHAPTER XXIX.

BLOOMSBURY

Edward entered the little vestibule of the select Bloomsbury hotel, and crossing to the office window, behind which sat a sleepy-looking book-keeper, asked for an envelope. Then taking a card from his pocket he scribbled a few words on it and enclosing it requested that it be taken up to Mrs. Povey.

A few minutes later he was following an attendant up the broad flight of carpeted stairs. It was then five minutes past ten by the clock which stood ticking sonorously in a corner of the landing.

*****

At twenty minutes to eleven Edward Povey descended the stairs and, walking quickly through the vestibule, emerged into Russell Square. There were but few people about, and no one seemed to notice the little figure which stood in indecision on the curb. Even had they done so it would have taken a student of human physiognomy of no mean order to read what was written on Edward's face. Some would have said that there was an expression of sorrow behind the eyes, others would have imagined a suggestion of a smile at the corners of the mouth, and on the whole countenance a look of joyful relief.

For some moments he stood, gazing out across the road at the lights of the Hotel Russell, and at the cabs and taxis that were drawing up before it. Then he turned with a little sigh, and made his way down Southampton Row, and along past the Museum into the glare of light at the end of the Tottenham Court Road. Here the sight of the restaurants reminded him that it was mid-day when he had taken his last meal. With the thought he crossed the road and walked up Oxford Street to Frascati's.

The supper crush in the great circular room had well began, but Edward was fortunate in finding a little table near the orchestra, and he prepared to order himself a meal in keeping with his feelings of the moment—some soup, a couple of kidneys, a kirsch omelette and a small bottle of hock.

He ate slowly and in a lazy contentment. At intervals his face changed its expression, now frowning slightly, now smiling. He asked the waiter who served him with his coffee to bring him writing materials, and pushed a clear space among the plates and glasses on the table. For perhaps ten minutes he sat deep in thought staring at the blotter, keeping time absently to a rag-time melody the little band had struck up by tapping his pen on the inkstand.

Then he squared his shoulders, finished his coffee at a gulp, and wrote—

"MY DEAR CHARLOTTE,

"I have been thinking things over, and I am willing to admit that I am not, after all, wholly surprised at the reception you gave me when I called on you this evening. But I may also say, that knowing you as I do, I was not prepared for the manner in which you acted.

"It appears to me that you might, perhaps, had you thought, chosen your expressions better. You could have been quite as effective had you been a little less vulgar, and you could have couched your suspicions of me in a less offensive manner. But let it pass.

"I can only surmise that the life of ease that you have been living for the past few months has entirely unfitted you for the management and duties of a home. I take it also that what you are pleased to term my desertion of you, accompanied as it was by ample provision for your wants, has not been distasteful to you.

"Perhaps you are right – that we had better continue to live apart. I am afraid that the future would hold many little rifts. Personally, I have led a larger, fuller life since I left England, and have seen many adventures (you would be surprised to hear that I still have a bullet in my back which I will carry to my grave). Yes, I am afraid our former existence would irritate me beyond measure. Your allowance will be paid to you as formerly. You need have no compunction in taking the money. It was fairly earned by bringing to a successful issue a difficult and delicate affair of business.

"Again, there would always be friction between us on account of our several acquaintances. I have mixed with the highest in the land, and could never tolerate the state of intimacy you tell me you are in with Uncle Jasper, a man I never pretended that I had the least affection for. He is a low fellow — and you know what I think of your Aunt Eliza.

"And so, Charlotte, we will go our own ways. The suggestion I made to-night that we should meet each anniversary of our wedding-day and dine together, I consider a good one. This will be a standing appointment, under the clock at Charing Cross Station, at seven, each third of May.

"I am glad to think that we remain friends.

"I am, dear Charlotte,

"Your affectionate husband,

"EDWARD."

Povey posted this letter at the office in Oxford Street, afterwards taking a cab to Victoria. Here he reclaimed his personal luggage, and had it conveyed into the Grosvenor, in which excellent hotel he engaged a modest apartment.

The taxi-cab which Edward had seen leave the courtyard of the station, and which contained Anna Paluda, bowled merrily up Victoria Street, across Trafalgar Square, and so on to Gower Street, turning off into a narrow and somewhat dingy thoroughfare which ran behind the Museum.

At Number 9, Dorrington Street, the cab drew up and Anna alighted. The driver had not particularly noticed the fare who had engaged him or he would have seen a vast difference in the woman who now tendered him a shilling and a half-crown, to the one who had entered his cab at Victoria.

The white hair which was so strong and noticeable a feature in the personality of Anna Paluda was now entirely covered up by a well-made wig of black-brown, drawn down over the ears, and a pair of slightly-smoked spectacles hid the piercing black eyes.

But a heavy veil made this alteration in the appearance of the lady very slight to the casual observer, and the chauffeur noticed nothing as, touching his cap, he restarted his car, leaving Anna standing on the pavement, her jewel case and handbag in her hands, looking up at Number 9.

It was a cheerless enough sight, dingy in the extreme, and the woman wondered that the fastidious Gabriel Dasso should have chosen such a habitation. But it was an admirable hiding-place, and doubtless the ex-dictator had only intended that it should be a temporary one. Who would think of looking for the dilettante fugitive among these sordid surroundings?

A few stone steps flanked by broken iron railings led up to a faded and blistered street-door that once had been green. The brass numeral under the knocker was hanging by one screw, and had fallen round so that it might as well have been six as nine. As Anna ascended the steps she caught a glimpse of a dirty area in which the street-lamp showed a littered profusion of bottles and jars. On a spike of one of the railings hung a tarnished and battered milk-can.

There was a semi-circular fanlight over the door through the grimy panes of which a gas-jet, innocent of globe, gave a dull glow. A light also showed beneath the blinds of the windows flanking the door-step. In the room within some one was thumping out a dismal melody on a cracked pianoforte.

The woman waited a moment to compose herself, then reached out and pulled the bell-handle. There was a jangle of wires, and somewhere at the back of the house a bell tinkled. The musician stopped in the middle of a bar, and there was silence for a few moments. Then she heard a door opened, and a shrill feminine voice shouted—

"Liz!"

Shuffling footsteps approached the door, a chain was unfastened, and the catch pulled back. Framed in the aperture stood a servant girl, small in stature, and of a dirtiness unbelievable. This presumably was Liz.

"I see you have a card in the window——"

"Rooms, eh, mum? Come inside, will yer?"

The small domestic stood aside to allow Anna to pass into the hall, then carefully wiping her hands on the torn square of coarse sacking which constituted her apron, Liz tapped at a door, and, pushing it open, motioned the visitor to walk in. Anna Paluda did so, and found herself in the apartment that contained the piano.

The room showed traces of a glory that had long departed. The furniture for the most part had been good, and was of that peculiar comfortless family of horsehair and mahogany with which the mid-Victorian epoch was blessed. There were a few pictures on the wall, one or two of which looked as though they might prove valuable could one penetrate beneath the grime with which they were covered.

There was an oval table in the centre of the room, from which the cloth had evidently been hurriedly cleared at the visitor's ring. Anna could see its crumpled dirtiness peeping from a drawer in the sideboard into which it had been hurriedly thrust. Glimpses of crockery showed beneath the shabby sofa, and over all was the same objectionable odour of meals which Anna had noticed even in the hall.

The person who rose from an arm-chair by the fire, and advanced a little to meet her, fitted the room to a nicety. She, too, was mid-Victorian, and, like her surroundings, had once been handsome. Her faded tea-gown was trimmed with still more faded lace, and faded ribbons nodded wearily in her faded cap.

Her face was pale and thin and worn, but there was a little smile which came into her pale blue eyes as she guessed Anna's errand.

"You have come about a room, madam?"

Anna nodded.

"Yes, for a few weeks—just a bed-sitting room. I want to be quiet. By the way, have you many other lodgers?"

"Two, madam; a lady on this floor"—pointing to the folding doors—"and a gentleman on the floor above. It is the room behind his that you can have, or one above it in the front."

"I think the back would suit me. The traffic at night cannot keep me awake there. Is the gentleman of quiet habits?"

"Quite. Mr. Gabriel is a foreigner, but he is most regular in all his habits. He is at home all day, reading, and he goes out in the evening. He comes in late, but we never hear him."

Anna followed the faded landlady up the creaking stairs, and gazed round as the woman held the candle up for her survey of the room. She did not take much notice of the furniture. The room seemed airy and clean, and she agreed to the price named without demur, forestalling the request for references which she saw trembling on the lady's lips by paying rent for a month in advance.

As she removed her bonnet and cloak she asked that a cup of tea might be served to her in her room. This in due course was brought up by Liz, whose appearance had undergone a slight change for the better. The new lodger made friends at once with the little maid of all work, seeing in her a possible ally of the future, and, without directly asking questions, she managed to get Liz to talk, and from her she soon learnt some of the ways of her fellow-lodger.

She discovered that Mr. Gabriel left the house about eight to half-past each evening. "An awful swell, mum; puts on a clean shirt every blessed night, an 'as one of them smash 'ats." When he came in the girl could not tell; they all went to bed and left his supper ready for him—"not much, only a basin of cold beef-tea, *consommy* ‹e calls it.»

"In his room, I suppose?"

"Lor' love yer, mum, not 'im—you don't catch anybody in 'is room when 'e goes out. 'E locks it up. I makes the bed and all that while 'e's there in the mornin'."

After the girl had gone up to bed, Anna sat up reading until the chimes of some near-by church clock told the hour of midnight. All was silent in No. 9, Dorrington Street. Outside, too, it was quiet, only sometimes a hansom would rattle past the front of the house, its bells jingling, and the horse's hoofs beating merrily on the asphalt.

The woman rose and looked out into the hall. On a bracket stood an evil-smelling oil-lamp turned down low. Beside it a brass tray contained the basin of *consommé* and a dingy little metal cruet. There were two letters there also, addressed to Mr. Gabriel, and Anna took them up to examine them.

They were in her hands when she started suddenly and put them back on the tray. There was the sound of a key being inserted in the street door below, and hastily slipping back into her room, Anna put out her light and closed the door.

She heard the man come up the stairs and unlock his door and carry the tray into his room. Then a match was struck, and with a start Anna noticed a thin streak of light break out in the darkness of the wall beside her.

She noticed then for the first time that the rooms, like those below, were separated by folding doors, but in the case of the first floor they had been fastened up, and on her side had been papered over and a heavy wardrobe placed against them.

Eagerly Anna Paluda placed her eye to the crack of light beside the massive piece of furniture, but she could see nothing. She determined that when Dasso went out on the following evening she would see what could be done to widen the crack in the papered door.

CHAPTER XXX.

REVENGE

A week after Anna had taken up her residence at No. 9, Dorrington Street, Señor Gabriel Dasso, as usual, left the house about eight o'clock. He had seen his fellow-lodger for the first time when he had passed her in the dimness of the stairs that night as he went out.

But the heavily veiled lady conveyed nothing to him at the moment, and the stairs disguised the height, which was so strong a characteristic of Madame Paluda. Dasso had merely raised his hat and passed on.

For some reason a bad mood was upon the ex-dictator of San Pietro. He dined as usual at an exclusive little restaurant in Soho, but his favourite dishes gave him no pleasure, and although he drank twice as much wine as was his custom, the black dog had settled firmly on his back and refused to be dislodged.

The hole-and-corner life he was leading was becoming very wearisome to a man of his tastes, and his long daylight sittings in the little Bloomsbury room were getting sadly on his nerves. As he sat over his coffee and cognac he asked himself whether all this hiding was necessary, after all.

It was only the memory of the man he had seen reading the *Imparcial* in Paris which had prompted him to this secrecy. After all, it may have been a coincidence. True, the man had also been seen at Dieppe, but perhaps that was another coincidence. He had certainly not embarked on the *Arundel* with him, and at Newhaven Dasso had noticed nothing suspicious.

No, it was absurd; in the morning he would leave Dorrington Street and take up his residence at some hotel and live a life more fitted to his tastes. Mozara's body, he told himself, would have been burnt out of all recognition in the fire—and ashes tell no tales.

Curiously enough, however, the woman he had passed on the stairs would come unbidden into his mind. Perhaps some turn of the head, some gesture, some mannerism, reminded him of some one he had seen before. Later, as he walked round the promenade of the Empire the memory of the woman on the stairs remained with him. He was drinking heavily to-night, and as he drank the depression he had felt earlier in the evening returned to him tenfold; something seemed to tell him that retribution was on his heels, and little devils hammered at the cells of his brain telling him that his hour had come.

He walked home to Bloomsbury, but the exercise in the night air gave him no relief. He was full of fancies—there were steps behind him—hands stretched out and touched his shoulder. Once he seemed to hear his name called. He cursed softly and told himself that it was nerves. He had no right to coop himself up in these dingy surroundings. It was life he wanted, rich and full.

It was nerves, again, he said, that made him imagine that a bitter taste came into his mouth after he had drank his *consommé* that night; perhaps that infernal Liz had put too much salt in it.

As he undressed, a curious feeling of lassitude came over him. He forgot his fears, forgot everything but that he wanted to sleep. He sat on the edge of the little bed and fumbled with unhandy fingers with his collar stud, but he did not undo it. With a little sigh his hands dropped nerveless into his lap and he fell back on the shabby eiderdown, his face pale and his breath coming in short, uneven gasps.

*****

In the night Dasso dreamed a strange dream. It seemed to him that he awoke to find the room hazy with the grey light of the dawning. Through the little crevices between the slats of the Venetian blinds the pale radiance edged its way, giving to objects in the room a ghostly and unwonted appearance. Between the man on the bed and the window there seemed to stand the tall shadowy figure of a woman, a figure which, as he looked, moved steadily towards him.

It seemed to Dasso that the woman bent over him and that two black piercing eyes burnt into his very soul. He tried to speak but could not. Then he heard a voice. The figure was speaking to him in a whisper, low and vibrant with passion, telling him what the little devils had been hammering into his brain—that his hour had come.

"—*your* hour, Gabriel Dasso, and *my* hour. For fifteen years I have waited for this moment, and I have never doubted but that it would come——»

The figure rose up and it seemed to Dasso that he watched her as she glided silently about the room. It seemed to him that she took up the basin which had contained his *consommé* and emptied the little liquid which remained into the mould of a pot containing a palm which stood in the alcove by the window. The whisper went on, and now Dasso told himself that this was Miranda's companion who was in the room with him.

"—and it is curious, is it not? that so experienced a conspirator as Gabriel Dasso, master of plot and counterplot, should fail to notice that his soup had, shall we say, a *distinctive* taste? Is it not curious that he should not have noticed that the lock of his door had been tampered with? You have been insensible some hours now—and you are bound and gagged. But you are awake, Dasso, and you can see what I am doing."

The figure came again over to the bed and bent down again above the bound figure.

"I am a woman of peace, Dasso, and it is no crime I am committing—only an act of justice. For fifteen years I have put the thought of vengeance out of my mind, considering the living before the dead. After to-night I will take my place again in the world, without regret and without exultation—I am a tragic figure, am I not? the mother of a murdered child.

"Any time in those fifteen years I could have killed you, you did not know me well and it would have been easy. But I *wanted* you to know me and to know why I am doing this. Perhaps God will let your agony be your expiation.»

The figure rose up and crossed over to the little gas stove that stood in the fire-place. In even tones she went on—

"I am turning on the taps, here, Dasso, and all the crevices in the room are stopped up. In a little while—when—when you are quite dead, I will put a cloth over my mouth and come in and cut off the scarves which bind you—they are silk and will leave no marks. Then

I will rouse the house and complain of a smell of gas, and afterwards there will be— —"

The vision of the woman with the piercing eyes grew gradually fainter .... and it seemed to Dasso that he awoke suddenly.

*****

The room was quite light now. It had been a bad dream. Dasso tried to rise—why, what was this?

His hands and legs were firmly bound and his jaws ached with the strain of the gag. The air of the room was heavy with the fumes of gas, and his chest pained him as though it would burst. In his ears were weird noises and he felt the sweat of fear wet upon his forehead.

Air—he must have air. The window near him seemed to mock him with its promise of life. With an effort he managed to turn on his side, and inch by laborious inch, he worked his way to the edge of the bed—then on to the floor.

He lay for a moment, breathing heavily, his heart beating in great blows against his ribs. He struggled on to his knees and began a series of grotesque hops towards the window.

But with each movement the effort grew more difficult and the strain on his heart grew tenser. Twice he fell forward on to his face, once he struggled again to his feet. The second time he remained lying where he had fallen, his head buried in the dusty fur rug beneath his goal.

Below, in the street, he heard the jangle of milk cans. Then a man cried cheerily to his horse and a cart rattled past the house. Some sparrows flew past the window chirping and quarrelling—they made a shadow on the blinds and were gone.

If only he could throw something and break a pane of glass. Air— air—not two feet away—and life— —

With a superhuman effort Dasso was on his knees again—then, a look of despair and a great fear came into the white staring face, and with no sound he rolled over and lay still.

CHAPTER XXXI.

A FINAL NOTE BY EDWARD POVEY

It may be a matter of some astonishment to the few people whom I number as my intimate friends that the records of my doings from the time when Mr. Kyser accosted me as I leant on the parapet of London Bridge, to the time I left the kingdom of San Pietro, have not been chronicled by myself in the first person.

To be candid, such was my original intention, and, indeed, I commenced the task only to find that it was beyond me. There were certain incidents in the record where my actions, however well they turned out, were perhaps not the actions of a strictly honest man. These (although I wish it to be clearly understood that I regret nothing) I felt that I could not write of without feeling a not unnatural bias.

I claim that in my schemes I did harm to no one; I will even go further and claim that I have been the humble instrument by which happiness and a splendid inheritance came to Galva. Had I returned Mr. Kyser's letter to America, it would probably never have reached Mr. Baxendale. If, in an after life, I meet this latter gentleman, I will have no fear. The case of the San Pietro inheritance, had I not undertaken the matter, would have been thrown into the hands of some unknown and perhaps unscrupulous lawyer who would have exploited the affair for his benefit rather than Galva's.

I do not wish to hide the fact that it was not alone the thought of this unknown girl which embarked me on my mission. I believe that beneath the shell of the most ordinary existence there is a kernel of romance, and it was this which tempted me.

I have always held that Romance is not dead, as some would have us believe, but that it is a question of environment. I heard a lecturer once say that Yesterday was romantic, and so is To-morrow, but never To-day—our grandparents and grandchildren, but never our brothers and sisters. Who can dare to say what lies beneath the most prosaic exterior? Where is the line which marks the difference between the man who drives his omnibus down Cheapside and the charioteer of ancient Rome? One wears a shiny felt hat, and the other, I believe, affected a fillet of gold in his hair. Apart from that they are identical. I once knew a man who wore side-whiskers and lectured in little halls on temperance, and I know for a fact that an ancestor of his helped to murder a cardinal on the steps of an Italian cathedral. But I do not believe that romance is dead in my temperate friend, it is only dormant. One of these days something will stir in his mind, and he will see things as they are, just as something stirred in me that evening I looked over London Bridge. I do not expect he will murder a cardinal, they don't do those things now. I know he feels secretly proud of his descent from his violent ancestor—the murder of a cardinal ages ago is so romantic—but should his brother shoot a curate, I think he would die of shame. Yet the crimes are identical. Why is it?

It is now two years since the events recorded in this book happened, and the proof sheets have just come from the friend who has taken upon himself the task of putting my notes into story form. With them, there is a letter in which he asks me to write a final note— to tie a knot, as it were, in the string of the tale.

I must pay my friend the compliment of saying that he has made good use of the data I have given him, and he has dealt as leniently as he could with my little failings.

I have spent a very pleasant two years, and I gather from Charlotte that she is as happy as I am. Perhaps, after one of our yearly dinners we will decide to take up again the life which was interrupted by the visit of Uncle Jasper. I hope not, however.

It is May now, a month which I always spend in the little cottage at Tremoor. Their Majesties the King and Queen of San Pietro, travelling as Mr. and Mrs. Baxendale, come to Cornwall also and spend a week each year. They will be here in a few days now, and with them they are bringing the Crown Prince, as sturdy a little Estrato as ever graced a cradle. I saw him last January, for I spend the winters in the delightful climate of Corbo. I do not stay at the palace, but find it more to my taste to take a suite of rooms at the Imperial, that new hotel which faces the bay near the Casino.

I rode out to Casa Luzo a few days before I last left the island, and it was with very mixed feelings that I gazed on the stucco porch and the little garden. I thought of Galva and Armand, of old Pieto and Teresa, and the ruffian who was wounded in the leg. The place has been done up, and is, I think, in the possession of a wealthy fruit merchant of Madrid.

Pieto and Teresa were well when I last saw them. They keep a small inn on the Alcador Road, and by Teresa's careful watching of the stock, the worthy pair manage to wring from the business a fair living. They receive also a yearly sum from the Royal Pensions list.

Anna Paluda resides at the palace. I often find myself wondering what business it was that really brought her to London with me. In my pocket-book is an old and much folded cutting from the *Daily Mail* which has put strange fancies into my head. One of these days I will show Anna the cutting and watch those great black eyes as she reads it. It is a report of an inquest and goes—

"THE DORRINGTON STREET MYSTERY

"*Yesterday Mr. Paxton, the coroner of St. Pancras, held an inquest on the body of the man Gabriel who was found dead in the first-floor room of a boarding-house in Dorrington Street.*

"*Mrs. Brand, the landlady, giving evidence, spoke of the curious habits of the deceased. Mr. Gabriel took the room about a month ago and had lived a very retired life, going out only at night.*

"*The servant, Elizabeth Harker, gave corroborative evidence, and spoke of the discovery of the body. She had been called at about half-past five in the morning by a Mrs. Graham, the lodger who rented the room next to the deceased. The lady complained of a smell of gas, and, together with the witness, tried to rouse Mr. Gabriel. No answer being given to their knocking, they turned the handle, and the door, to their surprise, came open.*

"*To a question from the coroner witness said that she had never known the deceased to sleep with his door unlocked.*

"*Further evidence was called showing that deceased had evidently destroyed all marks and papers that might lead to his identity. The windows of the room had been carefully plugged up and two gas jets were turned full on.*

"The coroner, in a few words to the jury, said that this was one of the many cases he had had to deal with of mysterious foreigners who met no less mysterious deaths in his district.

"From the evidence he should say that Mr. Gabriel was most anxious to hide his identity, and the evidence that he did not go out in daylight pointed to the fact that he went in fear of something. The deceased seemed to be of Spanish nationality, and the recent disturbances in Barcelona made one wonder whether this man was not a refugee or a member of one of the numerous secret societies, whose plans, perhaps, he had betrayed. It looked as though his fear had got the better of him at last, and that he had chosen death at his own hands rather than at those of his enemies.

"The jury, after a few moments' deliberation, returned a verdict of suicide. The body, if not identified by to-morrow, will be buried by the authorities

"A curious aspect of the case is that the Mrs. Graham who discovered the smell of gas has disappeared. There is nothing to connect her with the tragedy, but her evidence might have thrown some light on the affair. We understand the police, are making inquiries as to the missing woman, who took the room she occupied only a week ago."

The affair is now one of London's unsolved mysteries. Personally I have, as I said, my fancies—the date of the cutting is ten days after my arrival, with Anna, in London—but it is no business of mine.

It is peaceful here in this little spring-coloured garden. The sun has just dropped down behind a bank of storm-clouds over the sea and the lights of Pendeen are flashing out. A tramp steamer, miles away and looking like a toy on the broad Atlantic, is ploughing her way down towards the Longships. Perhaps she is going to Bilbao, or even Corbo or Rozana. Above me a large bird is planing on outstretched motionless wings in the copper blue of the sky, and the moors around me look like masses of crumpled mauve velvet in the darkening twilight.

And I—I sit here and smoke a very excellent cigar and wonder if Fate will ever stretch out her hand again to pick me up and drop me again into the whirl of things.

I say to myself that I hope not—and know that I lie.

THE END